INNATRAEA

Novella One: Small Footsteps

E.R. ZAUGG

This book is dedicated to my child Siri. I hope that you find the power of weaving dreams with your creativity, as you have taught me.

NORDRIA
ARAVUR ISLES
ANDRON
RIVAS
SOPHENE
THRACE
JENOWEIN
THIBELANDS
ALDONIA
BIN HSEDA
IMPERIAL SHENODA
FARUN DA'AL
EBRUNHA
SCROTAN
TURSIM
ROYAL STYLA
KINRA
AMNGEHOE
TLOKAH
INNATRAEA

Porto de la Luce
River King
BETHSEDA
RENOWHN TRIBELANDS
AEDONIA
Talberston's Crossing
Fairy River
The Shepherd King
Mu'zl Mountains
Haversfjord
IMPERIAL SHINODA
The King's Highway
Farmhold
Renfal Forest
Aliselle Falls
River of Flowers
ROYAL SEYLA

Table of Contents

"Every legend begins with the
small footsteps of ordinary Innatraeans."

-Tavid the Traveler

PROLOGUE:
THE THREE SISTERS

"Women have always been sacred to Innatraea. You can see our goddesses, The Three Sisters, in the sky every night, watching over us."
– *Crilla Sharone*

Rhiannon stared at the grove of Asherah trees outside her study window, enjoying a few moments of peace before her sisters arrived. The massive trees had been growing here for millennia, eventually reaching into the sky higher than most others on Innatraea. Their pink and white flowers swayed gently in the wind. Soon their delicious edible seeds would start to ripen.

Underneath the towering trees, soft grassy walkways traced throughout the grove. In happier times Rhiannon had calmly strolled those paths, and she wished she were there now rather than waiting to deal with her sisters.

The doorway to her study opened, admitting Selene and Serafina.

The Three regarded one another quietly. None of them wanted to be here.

Moving to her Mundukua or "world pool," she touched its surface gently with her fingertip. Ripples flowed away from it, borne by the tension of her magic. She lifted her finger away carefully, but not far, and the ripples slowly subsided, replaced by an image of Innatraea. She opened her hand, and the image followed the movements she traced above it. When she opened the hand wide, the image became more focused. The face of a newborn baby girl with curly red hair and brilliant green eyes appeared in the image.

Rhiannon regarded her sisters calmly. "I have chosen a Seed. This young girl."

Serafina stepped closer to the pool and looked closely at the baby. "She is powerful, almost our equal, nearly unheard of." Looking up at Rhiannon, she added, "Does she have a strong heart?"

"More to the point, does she have the mind?" Selene asked, more interested in the conversation than usual.

Rhiannon smiled. These questions were to be expected and she had the answers. "She is Sophenen; she is of an old blood line. The power she possesses is proof enough of her heart. As for her mind, she can be trained, and we have a unique opportunity." She closed her hand slightly, making the world pool focus onto a larger area around the baby girl. There, in an adjoining cradle, another baby girl lay. "Her blood and power are strong. More importantly, she has a twin sister. This opens up many possibilities."

Selene gave her sister a cunning smile. "Indeed, very interesting. Do we have a Vessel?"

"The Vessel would have to be a very strong one," Serafina noted. "I have not found a vessel yet, but we do have time," Rhiannon told them. "We could make use of Haitasi."

Selene, like Serafina, appeared mystified. "Do you think The Sacred Folk will care about our plans?"

"I believe that once we have shown Innatraea's need, they will have no choice but to help us. Especially if we approach the Amarok first."

Selene nodded. "I will do this. They are somewhat more willing to speak with me."

"Finding the Vessel will be my task," Serafina offered. "My ties to The People may prove valuable."

Rhiannon looked both her sisters in the eyes. "Then we begin. I will acquire a binding contract with The Siofra.

***

In the Sophenen noble family's nursery night was settling, however, it was not dark. Small, marble-sized globes of colored lights danced around the ceiling where the two infants could see them from their cribs. Both these baby girls could already weave, and both were expected to change Innatraea in her own way. Yet only one of them was the child the man sought.

"Hello, little one," he said with a smile, touching one of them on her cheek. "I'm going to take you away now, but don't worry. You will see your sister again. Meanwhile, I am leaving Siofra in your place."

The man carefully took the replacement he called Siofra out of his shoulder sling. The strange little creature clung to him with its lithe limbs. He smiled reassuringly. "Don't worry, you will have a family here too.

Everything is going to be alright."

The infant Siofra made a quiet gurgling sound as he lowered her over the baby girl. They touched briefly, and the infant Siofra started to change, its tiny body slowly shifting to become exactly like the baby girl. The man had been told it would work this way, but it was still one of the strangest things he'd ever witnessed, and for a moment it shook him. He quickly recovered and refocused on his mission. He left the infant Siofra in her new home and took the baby girl with him in his sling. With one last look around, he smiled at his success and left the nursery through the doorway that wasn't really a door.

Chapter One:
The Weavers

"Lasting power creates complacency.
This is the weakness of all institutions."
-Praeus: The Linguistics of Logic and Power

Crilla Sharone hesitated before the massive carved wooden doors. She rested her palm upon the engraved eye and loom of The Weavers, an ancient order of powerful magic wielders who lived hundreds of years and were able to alter the very fabric of Innatraea herself. She shuddered, imagining a life where she was no longer one of them. That very visceral fear, however, did not mean she would allow them to corrupt everything they had been. Even if she stood alone or faced exile, Crilla would stand. There was no other choice.

Sighing, she wove threads of air and loudly pushed the doors open announcing her entry. There was a time for quiet; this was not that time.

The expansive chamber was filled with every last one of The Weavers. Faces packed the balconies surrounding the vast chamber, all staring at her as she strode to the Greater Consensus' table in the immense chamber's center. Crilla slapped the ream of papers she held onto the massive table. One by one she looked each of the other Great Consensus members in their eyes. They all disagreed with her, but she was still a member, and they would listen. She would make them if necessary. "These changes are ridiculous! They will corrupt everything we are and lead to the destruction of Sceotan!"

Sister Sherielle Arsenault steepled her fingers under her chin and met Crilla's gaze. The woman was as beautiful outside as she was ugly inside.

A Nordrian, she was tall and light-skinned with blond hair and vivid blue eyes. "These changes will assure our power. We have all spent centuries building what we are, and these changes will allow us to keep it."

Crilla raised a single finger then lowered it purposefully onto the documents before her. "These changes will do no such thing. For a time, those of us in power now will not be challenged, that is true. But the legacy of these changes will create generations of weak children, not capable Weavers."

Brother Frederick Alwin had been tapping his fat fingers on the table, obviously annoyed. An older and overweight Aedonian with pale blue eyes and short brown hair, he spoke up now. "That is nonsense. How would changes meant to consolidate power cause the opposite?"

Crilla picked up the first document making a show of scanning its contents. "This one removes the ability for Lesser Consensus members to call for voting upon new members of the Greater Consensus. At face value this may appear to preserve your precious powers, because it prevents newer Weavers from voting you out. In the long run, however, this will prevent new ideas and create a homogeneous leadership that does not represent the Weavers as a whole."

Brother Deniz, their local Tursi bastard, waved a hand dismissively.

The thin, olive-skinned man, whose plentiful body hair made up for his bald head, was one of her least favorite Innatraeans. "Bah, that..."

Crilla ignored him and held up the next document. "This one seeks to consolidate spiritual beliefs under the Three Sisters. However, the instrument of said consolidation bans other religious beliefs. You will be asking young, impressionable minds to give up their faith while already trying to adapt to life on Sceotan. This will rob them of their spiritual identity, creating long-term weakness."

A clamor went through the audience. Apparently, Crilla was not the only one who disagreed with banning religions. Good. Wisely, the other Greater Consensus members remained silent as she continued.

Crilla held up the next document. "This travesty is not even worth the ink it was scribed with. Teaching initiates that obedience to the Three Sisters and rules equate to growth in power in weaving? Ridiculous!"

Sister Solange Mason, a dark-skinned, raven-haired woman from Royal Seyla stood up from her seat at one of the balconies and stepped forward.

Crilla pointed at her. "You are not a member of the Greater Consensus. Sit back down and be quiet." The younger Weaver looked angry but quietly complied.

Crilla turned her gaze to Sister Evelyn Atwood who sat at the table.

Thus far, she had been quiet. The woman was a classic Aedonian with dark brown hair, brown eyes, and white skin. She was also usually very reasonable. "What do you have to say?"

Sister Evelyn met Crilla's gaze evenly, always the balanced one.

"These changes create a more streamlined educational process for new initiates. There may be some challenges, but I think we will benefit over time."

Crilla slapped the table again.. "You of all Weavers should know better! It is your job to look after our initiates and their well-being!"

"My job? I am the priestess of Initiates, not you!" Sister Evelyn reminded her. "My purpose is to integrate new initiates into life on Sceotan, and this helps me!"

Sister Taia Mirzoyan, one of Crilla's oldest friends and a fellow Sophenen, spoke before Crilla could reply. "Much of this discussion has already taken place in closed consensus, sister." Her almond-shaped eyes held Crilla's in a way only one Sophenen could with another. "We are only here to vote on these changes today, in front of everyone. If you please?"

Crilla looked around the massive table at each of the other twelve members of the Greater Consensus. Many would not even meet her eyes. She knew the votes were against her. Even Taia, her oldest friend, would be voting for the changes. She sighed and closed her eyes, feeling a great weight settle upon her heart. A piece of her would always be here, but she could not stay for this.

Opening her eyes again, she scanned the audience chamber before taking the great eye medallion from around her neck and placing it on the table before her. "I cannot go forward with you in this. I will not stay to see you corrupt everything being a Weaver stands for." Her voice carried throughout the chamber, as the audience watched her, enrapt. What they were witnessing had not happened in recent memory.

"I renounce my seat. I will be going into retirement. I am a Weaver no longer."

She turned and strode out of the chamber to a roar of voices that only died down after the massive doors closed behind her.

***

Later in another section of Djelem'den, Taia walked out onto Crilla's balcony to find her friend sipping tea and looking out over the city. Crilla was a beautiful, statuesque woman and her height, graying black hair, and piercing brown eyes made her Sophenen features seem all the more intimidating. "Did you have to make such a monumental scene?" Taia asked.

Crilla eyed her sideways. "Would you prefer I just quietly left and let all of you bungle everything without saying a word?"

Taia joined her at the balcony railing. Once again she was reminded what nice quarters her friend had. Most of the city could be seen from here, including the harbor. "Bungle? Many of us are the same age as you, if not older."

Crilla chuckled. "Yet you act like children arguing over initiates like they are toys, ignoring the consequences."

"We are trying to protect our power from what happened with the new initiates a few years ago, all of those powerful noble initiates trying to take control of The Weavers, our tower, and Sceotan itself. We cannot allow that to happen again. The changes were all voted through, we stood in consensus."

"Changing generations of tradition and corrupting what we are in the process is not the correct way. You know how I feel; we are not going to agree. I am leaving, old friend. I cannot be a part of this future." Crilla looked out over the city again with sad eyes. "Sometimes I feel as though Innatraea would be better off without us. Maybe such power was not meant to last for hundreds of years in the hands of otherwise normal Innatraeans."

Taia put her hand on Crilla's shoulder. "I understand, though I don't agree. We have done much good together in our long lives, my old friend. What's done is done. Where will you go?"

Crilla went to her small balcony table and sat down, placing her teacup on a nearby saucer. "A farm town in Eastern Aedonia. I still have family there."

Taia joined her, suddenly feeling weary. "Aedonia? You have never mentioned the place."

"Did I not? It must have slipped my mind."

Taia blinked, there was a secret here. Crilla Sharone never forgot anything. "If you say so. I will make sure your quarters stay as they are."

"I will not be coming back, Taia."

"I know, but just in case. It will make me feel better. Maybe you'll have a legacy one day."

Crilla laughed. "Me, have a child? That is preposterous!"

Taia sighed. "I know, I just cannot believe you're truly leaving for good. I am going to miss you old friend."

Crilla pushed a small folder of papers toward her. "This is for you." Seeing Taia's quizzical look, she added, "Everything you need to remove

Deniz."

"Now? Is there a point anymore?"

"Do you really want that man, who led the aforementioned coup, as a member of the Greater Consensus? Especially after the changes?"

Taia took the folder. "That is a fair point. Though he will probably just run to Tursim."

"Probably. But anywhere else is better than him holding power here." Taia looked out over the now dark city. "Sceotan, and Djelem'den,

won't be the same without you." She took the small bottle of whiskey and two shot glasses out of her satchel. "A drink, between old friends?"

Chapter Two: Legacy

"*A Weaver's Legacy is an important and complex role. These young Innatraeans often inherit centuries of power, knowledge, and teachings.*"
-Amah: The Morals of the Weave

Gertrude Al'Shane put her basket of rose apples down on the bench and stretched her back. She was getting too old for farm work. It might also just be the weather. Apple picking season seemed to be much hotter than she remembered.

She saw something down the road. Shielding her eyes from the horrid sun, she saw that it was a horse and rider. Her husband, Jonathan, was in town today, but this area was relatively safe. She picked up her basket and headed to the barn to store her apples.

When she emerged from the barn, the rider she'd seen earlier was just entering the farmyard. Recognizing her sister Crilla aboard the horse, Gertrude smiled and went to go greet her. "I didn't think I'd see you for a long time yet," She said.

They embraced for a long time. It had been decades since last they'd seen one another. When Crilla finally stood back from her sister, she wore a happy smile. Still, there was sadness in her eyes.

Gertrude put a hand on her sister's face. "Your hair is grayer, and your eyes have more wrinkles."

Crilla laughed and also touched Gertrude's face. "You look just as old now."

Gertrude smiled. "Older. Farm life doesn't leave one much protection

from the weather. Now, why are you here?"

"They have decided to go forward with things I could not countenance, so I have retired," Crilla replied.

Gertrude blinked, genuinely surprised. "You did what? What did they do? It must have been something horrible to make you leave centuries before you wanted to! I'm sorry."

Crilla let out a long sigh. "That was a few months ago. River water down the mountain. I am looking forward to some decades of peace and quiet."

"I'll go put on some tea while you stable your horse, then you can tell me everything."

"Tea sounds wonderful, it has been a very long trip. Thank you."

Gertrude nodded and headed toward the farmhouse. Nothing else needed to be said. Were Crilla a normal visitor, she might have to point out where things were in the barn or give directions to the kitchen. They had been sisters for more than five hundred years, and Gertrude knew

Crilla was perfectly capable. She knew her better than anyone else.

Gertrude put the kettle on and started getting her jars out of the cabinet. Jonathan would have to help with the rose apples later; her sister coming home was more important. She laughed quietly to herself, though. He would complain about being old at dinner for sure.

A while later, Gertrude and Crilla sat at the kitchen table, cups of steaming tea in front of them.

"You still have your ring?" Gertrude nodded at the Weaver's ring Crilla had been absently fidgeting with.

Crilla looked up. "I could not part with it. I may not be a Weaver anymore, but some part of me still belongs to them."

Gertrude patted her sister's arm. "I understand. Try the tea. It's rose apple, almost like home."

Crilla held her teacup up to her nostrils and took a sip. "It is wonderful, thank you." She looked out the window. "Maybe I will find someone out here to teach someday."

"Do you really want to?"

Crilla looked back at her. "I do not know, truly, but I will eventually need something to do, and Taia put the idea in my head."

Gertrude smiled. "I understand. Now tell me what happened."

***

Over the next few decades, farm life taught Crilla the value of a simple existence. Everything made sense here. Everything had a clear purpose. Yet Crilla knew she could never be fully satisfied with such a mundane existence, which troubled her. She knew with absolute certainty that there was more for her to do than plant and sow crops and take care of animals for the hundreds of years to come.

On a particular morning she was enjoying one of her now regular morning walks and considering recent events. Gertrude and her husband Jonathan had rescued and taken in a Rinowhn woman named Chaya, who was pregnant and recovering from serious injury. They were powerless when compared to herself but still always helped others when they could, it was quite remarkable. Then an odd feeling made her stop in her tracks.

She had suddenly sensed Weaving nearby; yet no other Weavers lived anywhere near Aliselle Falls as far as she knew. She immediately headed toward whatever it was. If one of the Weavers had come to find her and ruin her retirement, she was going to paddle their backside, full grown Weaver or not!

Her eyes widened in surprise when she arrived at the spot from which the magic emanated. It was not another Weaver. It was not even an adult. It was a baby. The little one lay bundled in a small basket floating in the stream. The basket had gotten caught on some tree branches leaning over the water. Glow orbs floated above the child. The little marbles of light bounced around each other in the air as the baby girl giggled. But that should not have been possible. How powerful would a baby have to be in order to make glow orbs? The answer was staggering.

Crilla gently picked the little one up, after using weaves of air to move the basket close. The baby's brilliant green eyes sparkled with intelligence as they looked at her face and the glow orbs vanished. She touched the baby's nose and bright red curly hair, smiling. "Hello little one."

The baby giggled and tried to smile back. From retirement to adoptive mother in a matter of minutes, Crilla thought with some irony. The future she had been contemplating all morning certainly hadn't included mothering an infant. But she had no choice. The girl would not survive without a Weaver to train her—she was far too powerful. And Crilla was not going to travel all the way back to Sceotan just to turn the baby over to those incompetents.

"Well little one, it looks like our fates are intertwined. We will need a name for you. Something beautiful and strong." She thought for a moment, then smiled and touched the baby's nose. "We shall call you Rosalie."

Silently, Crilla thanked the Three Sisters for showing her at least part of her destiny. What exactly it boded for the future she couldn't guess, but she was certain she'd been sent here this morning to find this child. Raising a little one at her age would be hard, but this baby gave her new hope for herself and for Sceotan.

CHAPTER THREE: PRODIGY

"Those of greater minds and power must learn to wield them with caution. For they are feared by many."
-Praeus: The Linguistics of Logic and Power

Crilla laughed softly as she snatched the small hairbrush floating by her. Gently laying her hands on Rosalie's small shoulders, she paused to think before gathering the girl's tangled hair for brushing. Meanwhile, Rosalie squirmed in her chair.

"Sit still, you have made a horrible tangle of your hair again," Crilla told her.

Life was like this for her now: objects floating around their small cabin, different colored lights, sweets hidden in the shadows. It was almost unbelievable how much of a challenge raising this little girl was. Even at barely seven years old Rosalie already had the intellect of someone twice her age and an even greater amount of power. Crilla sighed, wondering if all children were this difficult, or if it was just Rosalie's power and mind. She had educated her fair share of initiates earlier in life, but none of them were like Rosalie. The young girl was one of the greatest challenges of her long life, but Rosalie would change all of Innatraea one day; Crilla could feel it in her soul.

"I want to play outside with Jonaas," Rosalie complained. "Besides, why does it matter if my hair is messy? No one else ever sees it!"

"That is not the point, child. You must learn to look proper at all times.

This is part of what makes a respectable woman."

Crilla could not see Rosalie's eyes, but judging by the tone in her little voice they were rolling up into her head.

"I'm not a woman, I'm a child, and I should be allowed to do what I want!"

"Speak correctly, Sharone women do not use contractions. That you are a child now is not the point. One day you will be a formidable woman and Weaver. What you learn now will form the foundation of who you become."

"I know. You always tell me that!" Rosalie's small face took on the look it always did when she was thinking. "I know you are right, but I still wish I could be a normal girl." The glowing orbs of light floating around their small cabin took on a different hue, reflecting the girl's frustration.

Crilla laid the brush down as Rosalie turned in the chair to face her. She knew all too well how hard it was being so powerful and intelligent at such a young age. Many Innatraeans would fear what this little girl was capable of when she grew older. Her manner of speech, behavior, and dress were about more than just being a proper lady. They were a shield that commanded respect. "I know you want that child, but you are not a normal girl are you?"

Rosalie looked down and did not reply.

"How you speak, act, and look will form the foundation of the way others see you. That is a part of what it means to have your power."

Rosalie looked up again. There were tears in her beautiful green eyes. "I know. It is just hard being this way." A small cloth floated over to her, and she wiped her face with it. "I will do better, mother. I promise."

Their eyes met, and Crilla smiled fondly, gently touching the little girl's cheek. "You know I am not really your mother, but I will do my best to make sure we both do better." She felt a tear trickle down her own cheek.

Rosalie smiled and hugged her. "I know, but you are raising me and that makes you my mother anyway."

Crilla hugged her back and closed her eyes feeling more tears building. "I suppose it does at that, my daughter. Now back to your lessons while I get the tangles out of this rat's nest of yours.

***

Rosalie winced in pain as another blow hit her cheek. She wove a different pattern of threads into her shield and tried to concentrate on the question. "The Great Loom, is the council that rules Djelem'den." She hated this training, answering questions while trying to shield herself from her mother's strikes. Rosalie was ten years old now and they had been training like this for nearly a year. Another blow slipped through her shield's pattern and she let out a grunt of pain, before narrowing her eyes and focusing back to what was happening.

Crilla smiled. "Good. What is it called when they agree upon a new resolution?"

Crilla did not move, but more little threads flowed toward Rosalie, shifting into the patterns of those painful strikes she hated so much.

Rosalie ground her teeth and began weaving. She would not be struck again! Her shield caught the volley of blows and she smiled, proud of herself. "It is called The Greater Consensus."

Crilla nodded, already weaving more threads into the small patterns of fire. "What is the body of all Weavers on Sceotan called?"

Rosalie stepped forward, pushing the pattern of her shield tighter and bending it toward the next volley. "The Lesser Consensus." An idea occurred to her, and she smiled. It would be nice to see how her mother liked getting slapped in her face for once!

Another volley came toward her as her mother asked another question. "What is the office where laws and contracts are written for Djelem'den?"

"The Cancellaria di Scrutati."

The volley of little patterns hit Rosalie's shield, but instead of dissolving, they bounced away, scattering out in the small forest meadow. She grabbed onto one of them with her mind, altered its pattern just enough, and threw it back at her mother. The small pattern of fire and air struck her mother's cheek with a sizzling sound, cutting a long gash as it faded from existence. Her eyes flashed with surprise and anger. She touched the gash with her fingers and drew them away. Red blood dripped from them.

She looked at Rosalie and smiled. "Doing something similar took me years of training and anger to achieve. I am proud of you, daughter."

Rosalie did not know what to say. Certainly she had expected a much different response. She arched her eyebrows. "You're angry with me, admit it!"

Crilla did not even hesitate in her response. "Speak correctly. I am not angry."

Rosalie raised her hand and held two fingers a small space apart. "You are too, a little anyway!"

Crilla touched the gash on her cheek again; the pain made her wince. "Maybe a little. I am still proud of you. Go along, you can go play with the boys while I make dinner."

Rosalie hugged her mother and ran off to find her best friend, Jonaas.

Chapter Four:
Childhood

Back at their cabin, Crilla set a large pot of stew to boiling and enjoyed a cup of lavender tea and much-needed solitude in her comfortable chair. She was thinking about Rosalie's lessons that morning. At one point, Rosalie had asked about the same thing that was on Crilla's mind: "You said it took you years to do what I do. Does that mean I am stronger and smarter than you were at my age?"

"Yes, but don't let it go to your head," Crilla answered. "You still have a long way to go."

Crilla inhaled her tea's aroma and smiled, feeling another sting from the gash on her cheek. It hurt, but she didn't mind. Crilla had done what she could for the wound, but most Weavers could not actually heal themselves. There were workarounds of course: providing more air and water to an open cut or even searing it with fire. But something in the grand pattern of Innatraea itself prevented a Weaver from affecting their own being. Maybe this would be a good opportunity to teach Rosalie how healing with weaving patterns worked.

She went to check on the stew, trying the fire's heat with her old hands. It was funny how in her old age she preferred doing things by hand, rather than using her power. Maybe a lifetime of taxing her mind had been enough, or maybe she just preferred the simpler life of a farmer now.

Truthfully, she was not really that old. Many Weavers lived beyond two thousand years, and Crilla had not even reached half of that yet.

Another thought occurred to her. Maybe it was raising Rosalie that made her feel so old and pleased with her simple life. Her adopted daughter was something to behold. Crilla had never imagined being bested by a child in training. Then again, there had never been a child like Rosalie, at least not one that Crilla had seen or heard of in her long life.

Raising her daughter was very challenging, even more so than most queens or kings Crilla had dealt with over her years. Rosalie was stronger than her, smarter than her, yet she was still a child in every way that really counted. The balance between teaching Rosalie and maintaining her composure when her daughter beat her at nearly everything was an interesting one. There was a fine balance between teaching and domineering, one that she had not previously understood.

When the tea was gone, she went to the kitchen to check on the stew again. She paused and looked out the window, still lost in thought.

Yesterday, she had watched Rosalie stop to say hello to Gertrude on the walkway. The child had gesticulated as she spoke, and her natural dramatic flourishes made Crilla chuckle. Back home Rosalie would have been called a choban, which meant "child of a shepherd," but was more accurately someone going and dramatic. That little girl had it in her to change all of Innatraea forever. Crilla sighed, as she felt that weight settle upon her shoulders anew. Their life here might seem like a simple thing, but one day her daughter would leave their small home to become one of the most powerful women in history. Rosalie, her daughter, the child she loved more than anything. It was Crilla's purpose in life to make sure she had the tools to do just that.

Their conversation at an end, and Rosalie happily tearing down the walk to some adventure or other. Gertrude was laughing when Crilla greeted her.

"You're turning her into a monster," she joked.

"Good. I hope she gives Sister Evelyn Atwood nightmares." "Crilla!"

"The Three Sisters saw fit to give me this young girl. I will see that she becomes a formidable woman. A strong will is as much a part of that as logic or power."

"Do you truly think sending her to the Weavers when she comes of age is the right thing to do?" Gertrude asked, her face suddenly serious. "After the changes they've made, it will be hard on her."

Crilla picked up a single pomegranate seed from the nearly full bowl between them. "Do you remember what I told you about power? That it is truly what rules the Weavers, no matter what laws or regulations they try to profess?"

Gertrude nodded, and Crilla held up the single seed.

"This is me. I am one of the strongest Weavers living." She dropped the seed back into the bowl that contained dozens. "That is Rosalie."

Gertrude's eyes widened. "Is she truly so strong?"

"She will be. Hardship is how Weavers grow. I will prepare her for them, and she will change Innatraea. I, like you, am a believer in the Three Sisters. My finding Rosalie was no accident."

Gertrude nodded. "I hope you are right. Honestly, I believe you are. I just don't like the idea of sending a child into that den of snakes."

Crilla picked up her teacup. "We were only eighteen when we first went there."

"But we had each other."

"True, but she will have all that I can teach. More importantly, she will have her heart, power, and intellect. I believe those will be more than enough."

***

A week later, Rosalie was angry at Crilla again. Every day was lesson after lesson. Remember this, do not do that, speak like this, learn faster, read that, write this. It was getting so all her mother did was lecture and criticize, and she was getting tired of it all.

After one such learning session, Rosalie ran to the barn and headed to the horse stalls without even closing the big barn door. She knew it was supposed to be closed, but she was so mad at Crilla! Every day was lesson after lesson. Remember this, do not do that, speak like this, learn faster, read that, write this.

She sat on the bench by the horse stalls and cried in frustration.

Sometimes she just wanted to play with Jonaas and Edmond. Why did she have to be a powerful Weaver? She just wanted to be a kid!

A small meow made her look down just as the white barn cat rubbed against her leg. She sighed and patted her. "Hello girl, how are you?"

The barn cat only came out when Rosalie was alone. Jonaas even said that he had never seen it before. She loved the small cat's spiky white fur and the way it always seemed to know when she needed its company.

She smiled at the little cat. "I know, you are right. It is not Crilla's fault that I was born like this, but sometimes it is so hard." She looked toward the open barn door and saw Jonaas coming toward them from the farmhouse. "Sometimes I just wish I was a normal girl and could stay here forever!" The white cat purred a few more times before running into the dark recesses of the cavernous barn. It seemed to always know when someone else was coming. Rosalie could swear the little cat was smarter than the others.

Jonaas leaned against the nearby stall door and looked at her. "Are you alright? What happened this time?"

Rosalie arched an eyebrow and put her fists on her hips in her best impression of his mother Gertrude. "I am quite alright Jonaas Al'Shane."

They stared each other down a moment longer then broke into laughter.

"You always make me feel better Jonaas."

His eyes shone with humor. "That's my job, the farm boy entertainer." He hooked his thumbs in his breeches and leaned back against the stall, trying to look older. Rosalie laughed so hard she started to cry, but it was the good kind of crying this time. She got up and started running toward the door.

"We should go find Edmond and play at the river! Come on Jonaas!"

***

Edmond coughed and spat out water before finally being lifted out of the river and dumped on the shore. Rosalie often used her power to get back at him when he was doing something obnoxious, and this time was no different. Using only her mind, she had lifted him off the ground and tossed him bodily into the deep water. In retrospect, it had probably been a bad idea to point out when Rosalie spoke incorrectly, as she was already angry. Throwing rotten apples at her hadn't helped..

Jonaas was laughing uncontrollably as Edmond brushed off the sand and grass from his wet clothes and joined his friends.

"That wasn't very nice," Edmond complained. Rosalie gave him a toothy smile. "You deserved it."

"You made her dress dirty; you know how much she hates that," Jonaas said.

"We're outside, we're supposed to get dirty!" Rosalie arched her eyebrow at Edmond. He held up his hands. "Alright, alright, I'm sorry!"

She crossed her arms and nodded authoritatively. "You're forgiven.

Now let's go find frogs!"

Jonaas jumped up, excited, but Edmond sighed. Hepreferred practicing sword fighting with their wooden practice sticks, but it was usually two against one. Rosalie and Jonaas were far too similar to one another.

"Frogs it is," Jonaas said without much enthusiasm "Do you think your mom will have a pie for us later?" Gertrude Al'Shane made the best apple pies.

Jonaas was already on his way to the reedy part of the riverbank. "Probably!"

"Maybe we can read after we have pie?" Rosalie suggested. "I want to hear about Royal Seyla again!"

Edmond rolled his eyes, but a few moments later he was down in the reeds with his two friends looking for frogs too.

CHAPTER FIVE:

JONAAS

Rosalie walked into the Al'Shanes' barn. "Jonaas?"

"I'm back here!" a faint voice called from somewhere in the huge structure.

She followed the voice and found Jonaas in one of the horse stalls.

He was on the ground petting a little gray foal. Once again, as so many times before, Rosalie was struck by how handsome Jonaas had become, with his light brown, intelligent eyes, brown hair, and slightly tanned muscles.

"Isn't she beautiful? Now that I'm thirteen my parents finally let me get a donkey of my own. Her name is Serra."

Rosalie set her book aside and sat next to them. She stroked the small animal. "She is quite adorable. You have always been so good with animals. I am glad you finally have your own to raise."

Jonaas smiled. "Thank you. I'll have to feed her milk from the cow and goats because her mother isn't here, but we'll manage." He looked at her book. "Doing some reading again?"

Rosalie picked up the book. "Yes, I do love reading. There is so much knowledge out there, Jonaas! This one is about the morality of your heart and applying that to being a Weaver. It was written by a woman named Amah a long time ago."

"You two!" came a voice from just behind them. "Always hiding in the barn."

They looked behind them and saw Edmond leaning against the stall gate. Edmond was handsome too, if one went for his type: tall and muscular with blue eyes and brown hair, and a singular love of swordplay.

"We should go practice our swords, Jonaas. Rosalie can read more easily outside anyway. It's a nice day."

Rosalie made a glowing orb of light appear above them. "I can read just fine in here, thank you."

"Serra is resting now, she had a rough day," Jonaas said. "I'm going to spend time with her. Maybe tomorrow?"

Edmond rolled his eyes. "Maybe your dad or Marged has time to show me a new form or two. You are both useless!" He waved at them dismissively and left the barn.

As soon as he was outside, Rosalie arched her eyebrow in his direction, and they heard a loud noise then a splash. Edmond yelled from the barnyard. "Hey! That's not fair!"

Rosalie laughed softly and opened her book. "I have no idea what he is talking about."

Jonaas leaned back next to the little foal and pulled out his own book, the one he always read, Tavid the Traveler.

Rosalie looked at him. "There are other books, Jonaas." "I know, but I like this one."

"Which part are you reading today?"

He flipped through the pages and put his finger on one, seemingly at random. "The part about Farundia and their old dragons."

Rosalie closed her book, leaned against the wall, and closed her eyes. Her smile spoke of peace and contentment. "Read to me.”

***

Jonaas stopped under a rose apple tree to gaze at Rosalie, they were both seventeen now, and though she was still the old Rosalie, in other ways she was not. She had suddenly become so beautiful.

A light breeze had come up. It caught Rosalie's hair, gently turning it over and making it cover half her face in a curly red wave. She moved it out of her eyes and saw Jonaas looking at her.

"What?" she asked.

"You're beautiful, I can't help it.”

She looked down, embarrassed. "Jonaas I..."

When she looked up again, he smiled and put his fingers on her chin.

31

She appeared nervous, and her eyes held a sensitivity. She opened her mouth, but before she could speak, he kissed her. For a moment it was awkward. Neither of them had kissed before, and he had surprised her. But their closeness had become a natural thing, as they knew each other better than anyone else. Her arms went around his neck and his hands found her waist. She moved back but didn't break away.

Their eyes met again. Neither of them spoke. He placed a hand on her chin again, and this time she kissed him. The breeze blowing through the orchard gently swirled the leaves around their feet. Eventually Rosalie withdrew, and this time she pushed away and sat down next to a nearby rose apple tree.

"Jonaas, come sit with me, we need to talk."

He joined her, a bit nervous, but this was Rosalie. He knew her so well. "What is it?"

She sighed. "Jonaas, I am seventeen now. It will not be much longer before I leave for Sceotan, to become a Weaver."

"I know. You've been preparing for that your entire life."

She looked at him, her eyes sensitive. "Staying with me for that is not simple. You would be giving up your home and your life to me."

"What do you mean?"

"Well, usually if a Weaver loves someone or they need a dependable bodyguard, they bond with them, turning that person into goddess bound. This bond, Jonaas, is forever. It changes you."

"I remember hearing a little about this. Can you tell me more about how it works? Has Crilla told you?" Jonaas asked.

"Yes, she has told me quite a lot and I have read about it too." She took his hands and looked earnestly into his eyes. "There are many good things. Goddess Bound are stronger, heal faster, live longer lives, and can sense where their Weaver is."

He squeezed her hand. That doesn't sound so bad."

"There are other things, though. I have to speak with Crilla more about it." She smiled. "I would love nothing more than to have you with me, but we need to think this through and discuss it more, alright?"

Jonaas leaned against the tree and put his arms around her. "Of course, we still have time."

She closed her eyes and melted into him. Jonaas sighed softly. He'd never met anyone like Rosalie. She was beautiful, brilliant, powerful, and had the biggest heart. She always worried about everyone else; who was going to worry about her? Was that what being a goddess bound meant?

***

Later that day Rosalie looked up as Jonaas' donkey Serra nudged her shoulder. She laughed and scratched her ears. "Hello girl." The donkey's contentment lasted only a moment before she began rooting around for an apple.

Rosalie looked over at the boys. They were focused on their swords under the watchful eyes of Jonathan and Marged. Nearly every day they trained with the wooden swords. Rosalie liked to watch from the barnyard.

She reached into her satchel, took out the apple, and gave it to Serra who inhaled it like she was starving. Rosalie laughed. Jonaas did not like to feed her too much, but Serra had a way of getting apples from nearly everyone when he was not looking.

She looked up at the boys again. By the looks of things, the sword match would be over soon. In truth, Jonaas hated swords, but Edmond loved them, so Jonaas practiced with his friend anyway. Edmond, on the other hand, did not share Jonaas' love for Shatranj, the ancient strategy game at which Jonaas was, oddly, a master. For every sword match between the two of them, there was a Shatranj match; that was the deal between them. They were good friends to each other, and Rosalie loved them for it. For a while she had been worried they would fight over her, but after her kiss with Jonaas, nothing had changed. They were all true friends, the three of them, and she hoped it would always be that way.

The match ended with Edmond winning, as usual, and she got up to head toward the farmhouse. Gertrude and Crilla would most likely have dinner ready for everyone by now. She watched Jonathan slap both boys on the back, congratulating them on a good match. The former soldier turned farmer was a handsome older man. Fit, with a short gray beard and hair and kind blue eyes, he had been like a father to all three of them though he was really only Jonaas' father. Having Jonathan in her life helped ease the pain Rosalie often felt from having no father, and she loved him.

Edmond appreciated the man as well, since he only had his grandmother. Both of his parents had died a long time ago.

Marged waved, wishing everyone a good evening, and headed home.

The muscular, red-headed, green-eyed woman was a mystery. Not very social in most ways, she had two husbands, and Rosalie had caught her staring at Edmond more than a few times. She was, however, helpful in sword training, being a master swordswoman herself, which helped Jonathan. Crilla and Gertrude seemed to trust the woman, so Rosalie tried to give her the benefit of the doubt.

At the house Gertrude announced that dinner would be ready within the half hour. Rosalie went to set the table. Jonaas tended to Serra, and Edmond left with an extra pie for his grandmother. Jonathan had to get cleaned up from the day's farming. Meanwhile, the two older women visited the old grave under the rose apple trees, as they often did. Rosalie did not know much about that, just that the woman buried there had been an old family friend and that her name had been Chaya. She watched the two women go. They looked so much alike, and yet were so very different.

Whereas Crilla was smooth skinned, Gertrude was wrinkled by the wind, and where Crilla was stern, Gertrude was more prone to smiling. Rosalie loved them both so much.

That evening back in their cabin, Crilla joined Rosalie at their small table and put down two cups of hot rose apple tea. The cabin was a little one, but cozy, and it was just the two of them, so they did not need much space.

Rose apple tea was Rosalie's favorite after dinner treat.

She closed her book and picked up her teacup, bbreathing in the lovely aroma before taking her first sip.

Crilla watched her daughter over the rim of her own teacup. Maybe she was not biologically hers, but the girl really was a miniature version of herself. "What did you read about today?" she asked.

"I was reading about Amah's opinion on bonding a goddess bound.

Is it true that some Weavers will bond without asking first?"

Crilla nodded solemnly. "You probably know all the basics. Goddess bound are the bodyguards and servants to the Weavers. The bond is permanent and has certain side effects. A much longer life, faster healing, a sense of location, and greater physical skills are a few. Most important, is their strong tendency to obey and please their Weaver, even worship them, often to the point of self-detriment. That fact, in my opinion, makes the act of bonding someone against their will the worst thing you can do to a person, because it changes the very nature of their emotions. Doing this without understanding, or without permission, forces them into a lifelong partnership they may not have wanted."

Rosalie looked out the window thoughtfully. "I agree, it is a horrible thing to do without asking first." She sighed and looked back at Crilla. "Did you know that Jonaas kissed me a few days ago?"

Crilla arched her eyebrow, amused. "Did he? That is interesting."

Rosalie smiled and looked down. "We talked about it, the bond. After talking more with you, reading what Amah said, and thinking about it myself, I am no longer sure. Jonaas and I – we are still so young. I do not think we can truly understand what it would mean right now."

"That is a very mature way to look at things. I am proud of the woman you are becoming."

Rosalie blushed. She was still terrible at taking compliments. "Thank you, I will talk to him about this again soon."

"You are not worried it will hurt him?

Rosalie looked mildly confused. "Yes, a little. But he has a big heart.

He is stronger than you think." "You love him."

"Of course I do. He has been my constant companion my entire life. There is no one as kind and honest as Jonaas." She gazed out the window again, a bit sadly. "That is the problem. I could not bear to see him hurt someone, to be forced to fight. He is not built for such things. Our pathways in life are different. Jonaas has his own road." She paused for a moment, thinking it over. "Though I think he may surprise us all one day."

Crilla arched her eyebrow at Rosalie. "Edmond is built for such things."

Rosalie laughed. "He is indeed. Edmond also has his own path. He will become a soldier and eventually a knight. I would not rob him of that dream. Also, I do not love him the same way as I do Jonaas."

Crilla nodded. "You are becoming wise in your young life."

A single tear streaked down Rosalie's cheek. She stood. "I am tired, I am going to bed."

Crilla watched Rosalie go. Rosalie was her daughter, no matter where she was born, or to whom. She was becoming a greater young woman than Crilla could have ever imagined. Raising her had been challenging. Even as a little girl Rosalie had been difficult, to say the least, but she would not trade those years for anything. The Weavers did not hold a single spark to Rosalie Sharone.

Chapter Six:

Love

"L'amore è la forza più forte che esista. Il cuore di un Innatraean è dove nasce il suo vero destino.
Love is the strongest force there is. An Innatraean's heart is where their true destiny is born."
-Royal Seylan Saying

Rosalie breathed in the steam from her lemon and ginger root tea and let it out in a quiet sigh. It smelled wonderful. Thankfully, tea was one of Crilla's few vices, which meant they always had wonderful herbs and spices in the house.

She took a delicious sip and opened her copy of Praeus' Linguistics of Logic and Power. A white glow orb appeared above her to read by. She truly had no idea how Crilla could enjoy her walks so early in the morning. She had asked a few times, and the answer was always the same: it helped her old bones feel useful. Rosalie smiled to herself. Chasing Jonaas and Edmond around town was enough exercise for her young bones.

The shutter of the window across the room rattled. She raised her eyebrow at it and put her finger down to mark her place on the page. The shutter rattled again. She rolled her eyes, lamenting the end of her peaceful morning reading, and gathered her thoughts. Then she wove a few threads of air, grabbed her would-be intruder with it, and lifted him off the ground.

She opened the shutter, knowing exactly who she would find there. "Good morning Edmond."

"Hey! That's not fair, put me down!"

"Do you promise to knock on the door like a normal person next time?"

He laughed. "Of course! I promise!"

He always promised to knock, yet somehow never managed to do it.

She dropped him. His face vanished from the open window as he fell on the ground with a rather satisfying thud. "Ow!"

"You deserved that."

He came into the cabin through the door and sat across from her. "What are you reading today?"

She bookmarked the current page, closed the book, and held it up for him to see. Edmond rolled his eyes.

"It is a fascinating book about the logistics of power and logic as they apply to Weaving," she told him.

"This is why you don't have many friends. No one our age cares about logic and power."

"I care greatly about both. I also believe that you and Jonaas are friends enough for me."

"Speaking of Jonaas," Edmond said, "we should see how his morning is going."

Rosalie picked up her teacup and took another sip. "I am sure he is checking on Serra by now. He always feeds and brushes her around this time. As for me, I am finishing my tea before I go anywhere."

***

"Good morning, girl." Jonaas patted his donkey Serra on the side and set a pail of water down for her. He scratched her ears and fed her an apple from his pocket. "How are you today?" Serra only snorted in response, and he laughed before getting out her brush.

The barn door creaked open, and Jonaas looked over. Rosalie's willowy form stood in the open doorway, her bright green eyes shining, the sun glinting off her curly, red hair. She smiled at him. "Good morning, Jonaas."

"Good morning, Rosalie. Where's Edmond?" She glanced up at the hayloft but said nothing.

Jonaas continued brushing Serra, waiting for his friend to jump out or throw something at them. When he looked up at Rosalie again, she was scratching Serra's ears. Their eyes met, and Rosalie said, "Do you have time to talk with me today, Jonaas?"

"I have been thinking about that a lot, actually." He sighed, but before he could continue, a stream of water landed on his head followed by some handfuls of hay.

"Edmond you fop!" Rosalie laughed.

As Edmond climbed down from the hayloft, Jonaas tried brushing off the wet hay without much success. In a moment, Edmond appeared, grinning ear to ear.

Jonaas gave him a dirty look. "You could have used dry hay, at least!" Edmond laughed. "That wouldn't have been much fun at all."

Rosalie held up her finger and twirled it delicately. Edmond saw, and his eyes went wide. "Don't you dare!"

Suddenly, the water and hay were floating off Jonaas and landing on Edmond as a mashed-up goop. He screamed, sending the other two into fits of laughter.

When he had finally composed himself, Jonaas said, "Now then, I was trying to have a conversation with Rosalie."

Edmond finished wiping off his face with a cloth. "You're always trying to have a conversation with Rosalie!" He pointed at her. "Don't you do it!"

Rosalie smiled mischievously. "I would never!" She leaned on Serra, idly petting her. "Now, Edmond, Jonaas and I really do need to talk. If you do not mind?"

"Oh, *that* conversation!" Edmond said. "I need to go clean myself anyway." He went away, leaving them alone.

Rosalie looked earnestly at Jonaas. "Jonaas, please allow Serra to go enjoy herself in the field and come sit with me." Jonaas did as asked, while Rosalie went and sat on the bench by all the horse stalls.

A few moments later, Jonaas rejoined her. The bench was small, so they sat very close. He took her hand and held her gaze.

"Rosalie, I've been thinking a lot about this. I love you, I always will, and I don't want to hurt you. But I'm not ready to give my life away to someone."

He looked down, close to tears. He felt her hand on his face and let her tilt his eyes back up to meet hers. There was nothing but kindness and love there.

"I understand, Jonaas." Rosalie paused, still looking into his eyes as though searching for something. "Jonaas, I talked with Crilla more about the bond. There is another effect that I was unsure of. It is the desire to obey and serve the Weaver." She cried quietly. It was a few moments before she could speak again. "Do you remember the wolf that got stuck in the fence a few summers ago?"

Jonaas nodded. He tried to give her a reassuring look, even though he was crying too. "Yes, I remember."

She put her hand on his cheek. "You would not let them shoot it. Instead, you made them wait, and you came to get me so I could use Weaving to release the animal safely." She stroked his cheek gently. "I will never forget that. You are so gentle and believe so much in freedom. I cannot bond you." Tears were flowing down her cheeks now. "You deserve a life that you choose."

Jonaas put his forehead against hers and wrapped his arms around her. "Thank you for understanding me."

Rosalie's face appeared so sensitive; more so than Jonaas had ever seen it. Yet he could not tell what she was thinking...

Suddenly, she was climbing in his lap, wrapping her arms around his neck, and kissing him. His eyes went wide, and he pushed her away.

She looked hurt. "You do not want to?"

"Of course I want to, but the bond. This won't?"

She laughed. "No! That requires Weaving. You are quite safe, at least from that." She wrapped her arms around him again and kissed him.

***

A while later, Rosalie stood up and smiled down at Jonaas. He smiled back and wiggled his eyebrows. She was glad they'd done what they had.

Still, there was no future in it, and that made her sad. She started getting dressed.

"Jonaas I need to go for a walk, you should check on Serra." Their eyes met. "This does not change what we discussed."

He nodded. "I know, but I'm glad we did it. When you're ruling the world from Sceotan we will both still have the memories."

She laughed. "You are incorrigible."

He got to his feet. She allowed her eyes to trace his body one last time before turning away to leave.

"Rosalie?"

She turned back. "Yes, Jonaas?"

"I know you have a hard path ahead of you. I love you, and I just want you to be happy."

She smiled a sad smile. "I love you too, Jonaas."

She straightened her dress and left the barn. She did not wait for Jonaas because she needed some time alone to think. Her emotions felt so raw. The weather was clearing up though, and the sun felt nice on her face; it was going to be a beautiful day.

She passed Serra, who was happily munching on a nearby shrub.

Seeing the donkey, so peaceful and content, made her glad. She wondered if she would she still remember this place in future years. Would it still be home after she was centuries older? Could she stand to hear about Jonaas aging and dying? She felt tears again, as she looked out over the farm fields. How did Crilla deal with such things? And what about Gertrude?

Rosalie hoped she could finally wiggle out the secret of why Crilla's sister was still alive even though she was not a Weaver.

She wondered what life would be like if she had been born a normal girl. Looking back toward the barn, she saw Jonaas patting Serra. He saw her and waved. Would she marry him and live in this small town her entire life? She turned back to look out over the fields again, and the strangest feeling came over her. It was as if her body and part of her mind were remembering something that did not actually happen. She reached out her hand toward the field. Why did she feel like there should be a doorway there?

She shook herself and started walking again. Oddly, she felt better, as though she had been through something and was now a stronger and more capable woman for it. It made no sense, but she liked the feeling.

On her way to the cabin her steps grew longer and quicker. She needed to talk with Crilla.

CHAPTER SEVEN: HOME

"Home is where your heart is born. Life is where your heart takes you."
-Tavid the Traveler

Crilla had just finished her walk and sat down with her morning tea when the door to their little cabin opened, and Rosalie swept inside. She sat across from her mother, her face a play of scattered emotions – sadness, happiness, confusion, and love.

When she looked up at Crilla she was on the verge of tears. Crilla laid her hand on Rosalie's. "Child what happened?"

"Jonaas and myself, we..."

Crilla arched her eyebrow. "Do you truly think that was a wise idea, with how things are now?"

Rosalie raised her hand to forestall further questions and looked away. This was her habit in recent years whenever she felt others were wrong or did not have all the facts. In truth, it was more than moderately annoying, but Crilla let it go for just that reason. She often laughed to herself about how much the habit would drive Sister Evelyn absolutely mad. "It happened after our discussion, and we both agreed that we cannot be bonded. I am glad that we were together, it was enjoyable, and I do love him."

So, there was more going on here. Crilla found this interesting. "Then what is bothering you so much, child?"

Rosalie looked at her, and the barrage of questions she'd been bottling up inside started. "How do you deal with it? Watching those you love grow old and die? Leaving home? All of it. Do you still remember where you were born, Crilla? Why is Gertrude still alive, did you bond her?"

Crilla blinked and almost laughed. Her daughter had always been like this. She would silently gather information for days then barrage you with questions, expecting an answer to every single one. Crilla truly wished she could see the looks on a few certain Weavers' faces when they experienced this for the first time. "Being a Weaver is truly a difficult thing. I had a Jonaas you know."

It was now Rosalie's turn to blink. Her eyes became inquisitive. "His name was Hakob. He was a climber, and I loved him. We used

to climb mountains together, just the two of us, to enjoy the view. My first time was on one of those climbs."

For a moment she stared out the window remembering Hakob's brilliant blue eyes, a rarity among Sophenen. She looked back at Rosalie. "He is long gone. He died over four centuries ago. But I still remember his face, my home, and those mountains. You will never forget the things important to your heart, they make you who you are."

"How do you deal with the loss? I am afraid..."

Crilla held out her arms, and Rosalie came to sit with her. Crilla hugged her close and kissed her on the forehead. "Your heart grows, along with your mind, and your power. Being a Weaver is hard; there is no easy way to deal with these things."

Rosalie laid her head on Crilla's shoulder and closed her eyes. "Why is Gertrude still alive, did you bond with her?"

Crilla chuckled softly. "I did not bond with my sister. Some secrets are important, others only exist because we do not know. I tried to figure out why my sister never died. I tried many times, in every way I could think of, but in the end I just accepted it."

Rosalie finally smiled, and Crilla was relieved to see a little joy returning to her daughter. "You truly do not know? That is ridiculous."

"Truly. Gertrude has always been a mystery."

Rosalie sighed and snuggled closer. "There is one more thing. Have you ever felt like you experienced something but forgot it afterwards? Like a feeling in your body and mind?"

"Once or twice. It is not a thing uncommon in Weavers' lives, though rare in one so young. When did it happen?"

"On my way here to see you, after I was with Jonaas." "Interesting. Let me know if anything similar occurs again, but it is

nothing to worry about. Many Weavers experience this."

She patted her daughter's shoulder. "Now, if you do not mind, I am going to check you, just to make sure there are no complications from you and Jonaas."

Rosalie nodded and Crilla started weaving. Oddly, there was no sign that she had been with the young man at all, which was to the good. The last thing Rosalie needed right now was a baby.

***

Later that afternoon, Gertrude looked up as her sister sat down beside her on the bench under the apple trees. She looked perplexed and a bit nervous, not a good sign. "What's happened?"

Crilla sighed. "Rosalie and Jonaas were together."

Gertrude chuckled. "We knew that was coming. I'm assuming you made sure there were no complications?"

"Of course, but that is not the only thing. They also discussed the bond, and both decided they should not do it."

Gertrude smiled; both of their children had always been so mature for their ages. Normally, cousins being together would be an issue, but these two were not truly related. At least Rosalie knew this. "I may have to tell Jonaas where he actually came from soon. I have a feeling that he will be leaving with Rosalie and Edmond."

Crilla nodded. She still seemed distracted by something. "That will be hard on you both, but it is the right thing to do."

"Yes. Yes, it is. Now what has got you so riled up?" Crilla sighed. "Do you remember the time instances?" "Of course, did you experience another one?"

"No. Rosalie did."

"You don't think she actually...?"

"I checked her, as I said, there was no sign of any complication, past or present."

"Good. That is interesting, but not that worrisome. It's unfortunate we were never able to root out the cause of those, but they never proved to be harmful. I still believe you were correct, that there's an unseen hand somewhere affecting both our families."

Crilla nodded. "I still believe that the person, whoever they are, is friendly. I just wish that we understood."

"I do as well, but we can't go chasing after it. That never proved to accomplish anything before."

"I know, it just bothers me."

Gertrude gave her sister a sidelong glance. "Everything bothers you, old woman."

"You are just as old!"

Gertrude smiled mischievously. "But less bothered. Maybe you need a husband. They are quite nice to have at times."

"The day I need one of those is the day I return to Sceotan!" "I shall make sure to bid you a fond farewell at your wedding."

The sisters eyed each other and burst out laughing. When Gertrude finished, she immediately became thoughtful.

"Out with it woman," Crilla demanded.

"I was thinking of our two families. Do you think Rosalie is somehow actually related to us?"

"That is interesting, though I do not see how. We were the last of the

Sharones – I checked extensively – and Jonathan did not have any living relatives when you found him."

"That would then imply that we're being observed."

Crilla sighed. "It would. That is what I surmised as well. But looking for them has, as we said, never accomplished anything. Also, they have never done us harm."

***

That evening, Edmond was sitting by the river wrapping the hilt of his sword with a bundle of cord Marged had given him. It was a bit sad to see the horse head pommel disappearing as he wound cord around it, but she was a retired knight and knew about such things, so he thought it best to listen and do as she said. Then he looked up, Jonaas was coming his way.

"Hey there, farm boy!" Edmond said. "You look tired. That must have been some talk."

Jonaas gave a nervous laugh and pointed at the bundle of cord. "What are you doing?"

"Marged said that I should wrap the hilt." He went back to carefully wrapping. "Apparently, my sword is special and will raise questions if the wrong people see it."

Jonaas sat near him and started tossing pebbles into the water. "Special?"

Edmond shrugged. "I don't know either, but I think she used to be a knight and probably knows about such things. Honestly, I haven't been able to ever get a straight answer on who my parents were, or where I came from. So I'm following her advice, just in case."

"Probably couldn't hurt. She's an odd one, but if she's right, then it's better to be careful."

Rosalie spoke from behind them. "Who is an odd one?"

The boys looked up. This had been the three friends' favorite spot since they were children. They could always find each other here.

"Marged. We were talking about her advice to wrap my sword hilt." He held up the sword and the bundle of wrapping.

Rosalie sat down next to Jonaas. She leaned against his shoulder but looked at Edmond. Edmond noted that her eyes were red. "I never liked the way she looks at you, I asked Crilla about her once, she didn't tell me much but I think Marged was Trefn Cyfiawnder." Rosalie told him.

"What do you mean? That order of women knights that was destroyed years ago with Cathyor?"

"You never noticed? She looks at you quite often, and in an odd way. Crilla and Gertrude seem to trust her though. And yes, that order of knights. I think Marged survived that."

Edmond looked over the flowing river in thought. "Nothing to worry about. She's attractive, for an older woman with two husbands, and I like that she's a swordswoman, but I'd much rather find someone my own age." He looked back at them. "I do wonder what she knows though, maybe my mother was one of them. Hopefully my grandmother will tell me more before I leave."

Jonaas threw another pebble in the water. "You like swordswomen?"

Edmond glanced at Rosalie. He was always unsure about discussing such things around women, but Rosalie had always been just another one of his friends. "There's something about strong women. The idea that she could be my equal and challenge me – I find that exciting."

Rosalie looked at the river. "I am pretty sure that I have dunked you into this very river many times over the years."

Edmond smiled. "That's different. Your kind of power can't be equaled by anyone that I know of. I'm talking about physical prowess, strength, and speed. Like a sword fight."

A touch of sadness came into Rosalie's eyes, and she fell quiet. Jonaas squeezed her hand. "Are you alright?"

Edmond felt bad, even though he wasn't sure what had upset her. "I'm sorry, Rosalie, I didn't mean to upset you."

She looked at them and forced a smile. "It is alright. I love both of you. I just thought about what you said – that my power cannot be equaled. Do you think I will ever find my equal?"

Edmond understood what she meant. "I haven't seen anyone. But Rosalie? We live in a small town, and we're leaving soon. Innatraea is a huge place; you will find him or her, I'm sure of it. Hopefully I'll find out about my sword and where I came from too."

His words made Jonaas look sad. He drew closer to Rosalie and wrapped his arm tightly around her. It was a tender moment, but moments like these would not last long. They would all be going their different ways soon, and Edmond knew it was going to be hardest on his two friends. He also knew they were both strong, capable, smart, and kind people. They would find whatever they needed in this life. They all would. He was sure of it.

Jonaas looked at him again. "From what I've read about Trefn Cyfiawnder in my book they were fearsome warriors. I think there's a chance more of them survived, maybe you'll find one of them who knew your mother."

Lost in thought Edmond continued to wrap the horse shaped hilt of his sword. Even if he didn't find out where he came.from he would become a warrior that stood for what his grandmother had taught him, and that would honor his history whatever it was.

CHAPTER EIGHT:
FAMILY

*"Teulu yn clymu ein gorffennol fel gwreiddiau coed
(Family tethers our past like tree roots)."*
-Old Cathyoran Saying

Jonaas sat down at the large dinner table, sensing an ambush coming. His parents didn't set out the large table often.

As they took their seats, the door opened, admitting Crilla and Rosalie. Rosalie sat near Jonaas, and their eyes met. They both knew full well what this was about, Still, it made them happy to be near one another.

Gertrude cleared her throat. "Neither of you is an idiot. You know why you're both here. We're also having a large family dinner, everyone else will be arriving shortly."

Jonaas glanced at his father, Jonathan, who quietly leaned back in his chair, a shot of whiskey in one hand. Jonathan considered such things women's business. His only contribution was a nod acknowledging his wife's statement. Jonaas found this amusing. Neither Gertrude nor Crilla needed anyone to acknowledge their authority.

Crilla had been tapping the table with her fingers, and now she stilled her hand and looked Rosalie's way. "We are not angry. In all honesty, we knew this was coming. You two have always been close, and a blind fool could see there are feelings there."

Rosalie nodded, looking unsure of herself. She glanced at Jonaas.

He smiled reassuringly. She smiled back.

Gertrude slapped the table. "Pay attention, you two."

Jonaas and Rosalie jumped in unison. Now Jonathan was the one who looked amused.

Crilla continued. "Again no one is angry here. We want you both to realize a few things, however. First, we know you discussed the bond. You are both intelligent and know that you are going down different paths in life. We are proud of you both for making the decision that you did.

"You also must know that you are lucky to be near a Weaver and to be one yourself. Otherwise, there may have been complications," she added, addressing Rosalie with her eyes. "However, Rosalie, you are leaving soon, and a Weaver cannot use their own abilities to heal themselves or handle complications. Therefore, this cannot happen again, especially after you leave here on that journey."

Gertrude now held Jonaas's gaze. "Jonaas, I know you're smart and that you mean well. Just understand that Rosalie has a long future ahead of her as a Weaver. You have to respect that. Am I clear?"

Jonaas nodded solemnly. He understood. Still, he was happy they had done what they did, even if he felt a little guilty about it now. "I would never do anything to harm Rosalie or her future."

Crilla turned back to Rosalie. "Child, we discussed this earlier, and I trust you. Promise me now that you will look after yourself and follow the path you are meant for. You and Jonaas have chosen different roads. This is hard, but it is time that you accept this."

Rosalie averted her gaze, and Jonaas saw tears on her face. He wanted to hold her, but he couldn't, given their present situation.

Rosalie looked back at her mother. "I promise."

A knock sounded at the door, followed by Edmond's voice. "Is it safe to come in now? We're here."

The older women both stood and headed for the kitchen. With his wife out of earshot, Jonathan called, "Come on in son, it's safe now." He chuckled to himself and went to the mantle to get his pipe.

The door opened and Edmond came in, followed by his grandmother Brianna, who went straight for the kitchen. Edmond sat at the table and regarded Rosalie and Jonaas. "You two look properly chastised, I bet that was fun!"

Rosalie flicked her finger in his direction. Edmond put his hand up to his ear. "Ouch!"

Just then, while they were talking, the other guests started to arrive. This dinner was more for Jonaas's parents and their friends than it was for him, Rosalie, or Edmond. The three young people were leaving soon, and Jonaas's parents wanted everyone together one more time before they left. The first to arrive were the Thanes, followed by the Crawleys, and finally the Llewellyn family. The men all stepped outside to enjoy a pipe with Jonathan before dinner, while the women congregated in the kitchen. This left the three friends to look after the younger girls, Rebecca Thane, and Maryanne Crawley.

Searching for a way to entertain the girls, Jonaas asked, "Who wants to go try to catch the barn cats before dinner?"

The girls jumped up excitedly and followed him out the door. Rosalie got up to go too, but Edmond spoke seriously, stopping her, "Rosalie?" She sat back down and stared at him, surprised at his serious tone.

"You and Jonaas? I guess I'm not really asking, it's obvious. But..." He looked more worried than surprised. "You think he'll be alright? I worry about him. He really loves you, and he doesn't have plans like we do. What do you think he's going to do?"

Rosalie had to think for a moment. "Truthfully, Edmond, I love him too. But we are going down different paths in life." She looked out the window at the barn. "I think he is stronger than you believe, though. One day that farm boy will surprise us all."

"What do you mean?"

She sighed. "I am honestly not sure; it is just a feeling I have." She looked back at him. "Do you remember that winter when the baby goat got lost in the snowstorm?"

Edmond nodded. "I do. Everyone gave up on it and stayed indoors. But Jonaas snuck out, found the baby goat, and camped under a grove of pine trees for two days, keeping it warm until the storm broke."

Rosalie smiled. "That is what I mean. Jonaas cannot weave, and he is not a fighter. But his heart and will might just be stronger than both of us."

Rosalie had to hide her amusement and joy. It was not often Edmond showed this side of himself; he would make a good man one day. "I think you're right. I always worry about him because he doesn't have plans, or the abilities we have. But he's strong."

Gertrude poked her head out from the kitchen. "The food is coming out now you two. Rosalie please come help; Edmond go tell everyone else." She disappeared back into the kitchen without further comment, knowing they would do as she'd told them too, in that Gertrude and Crilla were the same. They both went, as expected, taking a moment to smile and laugh at one another.

***

Later, when everyone was seated at the table enjoying their food, wine, and camaraderie, Jonathan stood and raised his glass.

"Hello everyone, thank you for being here this evening," he said, and everyone quieted down. "If you don't mind, I'd like to say a few words about our children, who will soon be venturing away from home and becoming young adults.Jonaas, my son, I'm proud of the man you are becoming."

He raised his glass toward Jonaas. Rosalie saw tears welling in Jonaas' eyes, and it made her smile. Jonaas always felt so much.

"But I've had more than my fair share of seeing all three of these children grow up," Jonathan continued. "Rosalie. Edmond. Jonaas. All three of you are amazing. It's been a pleasure watching you grow up and become the people you are."

He paused as if searching for words. Gertrude quickly stood and put her hand on his shoulder.

"We truly hope you succeed and find happiness, though we will miss you," Gertrude told the three friends. Aliselle Falls will never be the same without you, and you are always welcome home. But please always remember to seek what makes you happy, that is what we all want for you."

She and Jonathan sat back down. Jonathan glanced at her gratefully.

Crilla stood up next. She held Rosalie's gaze for a moment before addressing the three as a group.

"Each of you possesses the best of us in your own unique way. I expect we will be seeing great things from you all in the future. Please remember to take care of yourselves and each other. I have faith in you always." She briefly met Rosalie's gaze before sitting down.

Across the table, a tear flowed down Rosalie's cheek.

***

Later that night, after everyone had left, Jonaas joined his father who had just finished smoking his evening pipe on the porch. His father smiled at him reassuringly. "Being in love with a Sharone is no easy thing for any man, son. You have done well."

Jonaas sighed and looked out across the farmyard. He hoped to catch a glimpse of Rosalie before she disappeared around the bend on her way home with Crilla, but she was already too far away. He appreciated his father's words and knew he'd made the right choice, but that didn't make things any easier. "I know. Rosalie has always been so much stronger than me, but she has never treated me differently because of it." He looked at his father then back out across the farmyard again. "But I still worry about her, even as strong as she is."

His father finished tapping out his pipe's dottle and started packing it again before replying. "Explain that line of thought to me, son."

"Rosalie's powerful, smart, and kind, but I think she needs people more than she realizes," Jonaas said. "We talked about that a little when we discussed the bond, and I've heard Crilla warn her about the Jhorian military when she leaves home." He looked at his father. "Do you think she will find someone as strong as she is? Who can protect her the way she needs?"

His father lit the tobacco and blew smoke into the night air before replying. "You have been thinking about this a lot, and that's good son. A man should think and consider his choices carefully in life. The Jhorians are indeed a worry, they are not kind to Weavers." He looked out over the farm field and his eyes took on a look of memory, with just a touch of sadness. "I have seen such myself. They don't believe that anyone but their god, Jhoras, should wield that kind of power, especially a woman. It's very unfortunate that they have such a strong alliance here with the Aedonian king." He squeezed Jonaas' shoulder. "But Crilla's trained her for this.

Rosalie knows what to look out for and how to be careful. The best thing you can do for Rosalie now is to look out for her until she's in a ship headed for Sceotan. "Don't let her know, though. Sharone women hate being looked after."

In spite of the serious matter at hand, Jonaas found himself smiling. "You're right, Rosalie definitely hates that. Sometimes she needs it, though."

"They all do, son. I'll never admit to saying this, but I think that's what a Goddess Bound is, someone who looks after their Weaver. The bond allows them to overlook their need to do everything alone and accept help."

Jonaas felt tears forming, and he closed his eyes, trying not to let them spill out. "When we first talked about the bond, I thought that's what I wanted. To look after Rosalie. But for some reason I just couldn't do it."

"You remind me a lot of myself at your age Jonaas. I'm honestly glad that you're taking a different road in life. I think it will be better for you."

"What do you mean?"

His father looked out into the night with a faraway expression. "When I first left home it was hard, too. The world is a big place and I loved Cathyor. But my heart belonged somewhere else. I was a wanderer." You have that wanderlust in you too, Jonaas, it's why you love that book so much and why you couldn't be bonded." He turned back toward the house and opened the door. "Come on son, it's late. There will be other women.

Love isn't limited to one person even if we think so at the time."

CHAPTER NINE:
HEARTBREAK

Rosalie sipped her tea and sighed. In the weeks since the large family gathering, moments of peace and quiet like this had become rare. Crilla especially liked to invade Rosalie's time and space. Even now she could hear Crilla in her head. "What is this weave? Who is this sister? What is this called? How do you do that? What do you do if this happens? What is your plan for that?" Truthfully, her whole childhood had been this way, but recently the grilling had increased.

Jonaas and Edmond felt it too. Everyone knew the three friends were leaving soon. You could hear it in their voices, see it in their glances, and sense it in all those little things that were not exactly conscious but definitely there.

She sighed and closed her eyes for a moment. There was also the thing between her and Jonaas to deal with. They both knew the decision was made, that their paths were different, and that they were not supposed to be together again. But goddess, she still wanted to be with him. When he moved a certain way, said a certain thing, looked at her the way he did, or any number of similar things, she was reminded just how much she wanted him. Just thinking about it made her shiver, which was beyond irritating because it defied all of her plans.

She opened her eyes again, set her teacup down, and closed her book. She looked at the window shutter. It did not move. She drummed her fingers on the cover of her book. The shutter still did not move. Finally, she used a few threads of air to open the window shutter and looked outside.

Edmond was not there, yet he should have been. Had something happened on his way here? Was he helping Brianna with something? She put her book down and got up to go check. Better to go look for him than sit there wondering.

Edmond's cabin that he shared with his grandmother was not far, but Rosalie found her thoughts wandering as she walked anyway. So much was changing soon that she could not help thinking about it all constantly. She would be leaving her home, Crilla, Jonaas, her friends, and going to The Weavers. Innatraea was a vast world and she was excited to see it, but there was much to be afraid of too. As she neared their cabin Rosalie shook herself, because Edmond was there standing in the middle of the road.

There he stood, motionless. She called to him, "Edmond?" Still, he did not move or reply. Something wasn't right.

She walked faster, and when she reached him she saw he was crying. She placed a hand on his shoulder. "Edmond what has happened?"

"She's gone." He looked at their small cabin.

Oh no, not Brianna, Rosalie thought. She held out her arms. "Come here."

He came to her, and she held him while he cried. "What do you need? Name it."

"Help me get my things," he choked. "Brianna, she was Cathyoran." He pulled away and looked back at the cabin.

"She told me that they burn their loved ones after death Will you help me?"

"Of course I will. You just stay here."

She patted his shoulder and went inside. Brianna lay there on her bed, silent, as if sleeping. Rosalie gently covered the old woman with a blanket, letting her hand linger a moment, then she got Edmond's things. They were easy to find – only a pack and his sword. Apparently, he had been ready to go for days.

Rosalie brought him his things and set them down. "Do you want to say anything?"

He nodded. To the cabin, he said, "I love you grandmother, thank you for everything."

Rosalie put her hand on his shoulder and squeezed gently. Then she wove threads of fire around the small cabin, turning it into a funeral pyre. "Goodbye Brianna, may you find peace in the next world."

"She wasn't really my grandmother," Edmond said sounding quite matter of fact.

She looked at him. "What are you talking about?"

"She told me last night after we got home. It's like she knew it was her last chance. She said she was my family's nursemaid before they were all killed. She also warned me to keep my birthmark covered and be careful. Rosalie, I don't know who I am."

"Edmond, you are our friend and a good man, that is all that matters." They stood for a long time, silently watching the small cabin burn.

When the roof finally collapsed, he said, "Rosalie, I need to leave." "I know."

"Come on, let's go find Jonaas."

Edmond picked up his things and they started walking, each quietly lost in their own thoughts. On their way to the barnyard they looked for Jonaas. He should have been in one of the fields with Serra this time of day, but the fields were empty.. They checked the barn. He was not there either, but Serra was in her stall, so Rosalie got the donkey an apple.

Rosalie was starting to get a sinking feeling inside. Where was he?

"We should go check the apple orchard. I do not know where else to look besides the farmhouse, and I cannot imagine he would still be sleeping this late."

Edmond put his things down inside the barn. He was still on edge and red-eyed, but finding Jonaas gave him something to do. "Let's go."

They found Jonaas in the apple orchard. Oddly, he was kneeling by the old grave that Gertrude and Crilla often visited. When they got closer she heard him sobbing, and her heart sank. Jonaas too? What now?

She knelt by him. "Jonaas?"

He looked at her and reached out his hand to her. She offered her own hand, and he lay something in her open palm. It was a beautiful rough stone pendant, lined with veins of blue, gold and purple, tied on a leather cord.

"They're not my parents," he said, his voice hitching.

Rosalie could not conceal her shock. Both of them? On the same day? "What do you mean?"

Jonaas looked at the grave. More tears ran down his face.

"The gravestone belonged to her, Chaya. She was my mother, she was Rinowhn. They told me she'd been attacked, and they saved her. Then she gave birth to me. That means I was born because someone did that to her."

Rosalie wrapped her arms around Jonaas. She looked toward the farmhouse and saw Gertrude. Crilla and Jonathan were there too. Anger boiled deep within her. Why hadn't they told Jonaas sooner? Why wait until now? She stroked his hair gently. Her poor farm boy.

"Jonaas, that tragedy does not make you who you are. How you live does that. You are a good person, you have a beautiful heart, you are our friend and my first love."

Edmond joined them, and they kneeled together for a long time, holding one another, and crying together. After a while, Jonaas spoke quietly. "I want to leave. A part of me doesn't belong here anymore."

"Me too," Edmond said. It's time for us to go."

"We will sleep in the hayloft tonight, the three of us, like we used to when we were children," Rosalie said. "Then tomorrow we will leave together."

She kissed them on their foreheads and held them tighter.

***

Later that night, Gertrude quietly climbed up to the hayloft and looked in on the three children. Her son and Edmond were fast asleep on either side of Rosalie, their heads cradled in her arms. Rosalie, however, was wide awake, and when her eyes met Gertrude's, there was anger in them.

"Not telling Jonaas for so long was selfish and very unkind of you," Rosalie said.

Gertrude was taken aback but quickly recovered. "You presume to tell me how to parent my own son?"

Rosalie's eyes smoldered in a way Gertrude had never seen before. "He is not your son though, is he? Crilla told me as a child that she found me, and I have had a good life. The choice you made broke Jonaas's heart."

"I only ever meant to protect him, I never wanted to hurt him. I love Jonaas like he is my own son. I raised him as such."

"If you truly only wanted to protect Jonaas then you would have told him. He would have spent his life knowing that you loved him enough to rescue him from what caused his birth. Hiding it was selfish and made him feel ashamed of who he is." Tears had begun trickling down her cheeks, dousing the flames. "We are leaving tomorrow. The three of us, all together."

Gertrude nodded. She, too, had begun to cry. "I understand. We will get everything ready." She looked at her son again, laying in Rosalie's arms, asleep. She loved him so much; she had never meant to hurt him.

There was nothing else to say. Gertrude quietly climbed back down the ladder and went to the farmhouse where she found Crilla and Jonathan at the kitchen table. She sat next to her husband.

"They're leaving tomorrow," Gertrude said, her voice hitching. "Jonaas is heartbroken, and Rosalie is furious. I think we made a very big mistake not telling him sooner."

Jonathan put his hand on hers. "Learning hard truths can be difficult.

Let's hope he heals and decides to come home one day."

Crilla nodded, her face calm as always. "I saw Brianna's cabin earlier. With Jonaas learning the truth today as well, I am certain both of them will want to leave. Their lives are no longer tied to this place."

"I'm sure neither of them feels at home here anymore," Jonathan agreed. "I understand that feeling. We have to let them go."

Crilla addressed Gertude directly. "He is strong and will be alright. I believe he will come to understand why you did not tell him. Though, if you are honest with yourself, there was more than a bit of selfishness involved on your part."

"Crilla's right, but Jonaas knows we love him," Jonathan said. "You explained your reasoning, now just give him time."

Gertrude managed a smile. She still felt sad and angry at herself, but she felt confident time would heal her son. "We need to get everything ready for them to leave tomorrow."

CHAPTER TEN:
DEPARTURE

That night Rosalie slept fitfully, lost between her worries and dreams about the future. Would the boys be alright without her? Would she be strong enough to travel across Innatraea on her own and join The Weavers? How would she handle living for centuries, long after her friends, the ones she truly loved, had passed away? Why had she been born with such power? Most terrifying of all, though, was a dream in which she grew up a normal girl in Aliselle Falls, married Jonaas, had babies, and eventually died an old woman. That life did not feel right at all; she was meant to be someone else.

The next morning, Rosalie woke to the gentle warmth of sunlight and animal fur on her face. She opened her eyes and smiled. Reaching out, she petted the spiky-haired white barn cat.

"Hello, old friend, I have not seen you in a long time."

The little cat's only response was to run its face against her and purr.

"You always seem to know when I need you."

Their eyes met, making Rosalie smile again. "I know everything will be alright. I just worry sometimes."

A noise from below startled the little barn cat, and she ran off. The boys were already up, and by the sound of it, they were already getting ready. She sat up and stretched, still tired. Yesterday had been long and trying, followed by a long night with little sleep. Hopefully the boys had fared better.

She got up and climbed down from the hayloft. They were there, loading a small old wooden cart and preparing Serra to be hitched to it. Jonathan saw her and quietly retreated from the barn, leaving her alone with Jonaas and Edmond.

"Good morning," Rosalie greeted them.

Jonaas looked tired still, but in much better spirits. "Good morning Rosalie! We're almost ready, we didn't want to wake you."

Edmond looked tired as well. "They got most of the things we needed ready last night. I don't know what you said, but it worked."

Rosalie remembered her short conversation with Gertrude. Mistakes and selfishness aside, the Al'Shanes were good people, and they knew what was happening.

"Good, the sooner we get going the more we can walk. I am glad you are both coming too; it will be easier for all three of us that way. I love both of you, I want you both to be happy."

Edmond smiled. "I love you both, too." Then, to Rosalie's surprise, he took Serra's reins and led the donkey out of the barn with the newly hitched cart, leaving Rosalie and Jonaas alone together.

Jonaas looked at her with his innocent farm boy eyes that she loved so much. "It's almost time to go."

Rosalie went to him, hung the rough stone pendant around his neck, and put her hand on his face. "Almost, but not yet." She looked back at the horse stalls. "I will always remember that. And you. No matter what happens."

He wrapped his arms around her from behind and kissed her on the head. "I will too. Come on, let's go say goodbye to everyone."

She leaned against him. "Not yet. Hold me a little longer."

A little later, Rosalie turned and faced him squarely. She kissed him long and soft. "Now it is time to go."

They walked together out of the barn and into the morning sunlight where everyone was waiting. Edmond saw them and waved. He and Serra were near the old cart path that led to the town's main road and beyond that the King's Highway. Jonathan had just finished talking to him, and now he came over to Rosalie and Jonaas. Crilla and Gertrude were there as well. Rosalie went straight to Crilla and hugged her.

"I am sorry this was so abrupt," Rosalie told her adopted mother. "I will miss you dearly. Thank you for everything; my life would not have been the same without you."

"You were the best thing in my long life, and I love you," Crilla said. "You are my legacy, and I have complete faith in who you are. Remember to be careful of the Jhorian Crows. Those inquisitors look for Weavers, and you are not hiding at home any longer. There is a very big difference between the Aedonian military Edmond plans to enlist with and that of the Jhorian faith. Go straight to Haversfjord and do your best to find a ship from there. Leaving Aedonia quickly is your best chance of going unnoticed by The Crows. May the Goddesses keep you safe on your journey." She kissed Rosalie on the forehead. "Remember everything I have taught you, and always do your best."

Rosalie hugged her again. "I love you too. I will remember your instructions and be careful, I promise. One day I will come back and tell you everything. Goddesses keep you safe until then."

As the two spoke, Jonathan joined Gertrude and Jonaas who were engaged in serious conversation of their own.

"I am sorry that I did not tell you earlier, son, that was selfish of me," Gertrude was saying. "She looked at Jonathan with a bittersweet expression. "Jonathan and I were never able to conceive, so you were our miracle. I know how awful that sounds, but it's the truth."

"I understand," Jonaas told her. "I'm not angry exactly; maybe disappointed and sad." He looked around the farmyard and at the barn. "Even though I grew up here, all of a sudden I feel like a part of myself belongs somewhere else. But you'll always be my parents. I'm not leaving because I'm angry; I'm leaving because I need to find out where I belong."

Jonathan said, "We understand, son, better than you know. Be safe and know that you'll always have a home here. Come back and tell me about your adventures someday."

It was time for the two young travelers to go. Crilla picked up Rosalie's satchel and handed it to her. It was heavier than usual, and it clinked as Rosalie took it.

"There are marks enough in there for your journey," Crilla told Rosalie. "Also, your two favorite books and a few royal scripts you can use in any large city. The most important are the last two items They are a letter to an old friend of mine in Djelem'den on Sceotan, and this." She held out a chain on which hung her patterned Weaver's ring. She put it around Rosalie's neck. "The ring will have to attune itself to you before you can wear it, but in time it will. Keep it close."

Rosalie thanked Crilla then turned to Gertrude. "I love you, and I am sorry for my sharp tongue last night. But I still feel the way that I do. I love him, and I hate to see him hurt by anyone, even you."

Gertrude nodded. " I will never be angry with you for protecting Jonaas. Be safe Rosalie. May the Goddesses carry you."

They hugged, though a bit awkwardly. Jonathan hugged her too.

"Be safe, Rosalie, and depend upon the boys until you're safely out of Aedonia," he said. You will always have a home here, too." To Jonaas he said, "My old infantry sword is in the cart, along with food, water, and some marks. Be safe, son. I love you. Make sure that it's you or Edmond who speak with any soldiers you see."

Jonaas hugged his parents one last time. "I love you both. I'll come home again one day."

Gertrude kissed him on the forehead. "We love you too, son, be careful and come back to us."Rosalie and Jonaas joined Edmond. The three friends waved one last time and started down the old cart path, Serra pulling the cart alongside. Rosalie smiled to herself; her journey had finally begun.

None of them noticed the little white barn cat watching them from the barn's hay door.

CHAPTER ELEVEN:
THE KING'S HIGHWAY

"Innatraea is as harsh as she is beautiful."
-Tavid the Traveler

A few days later Rosalie stared into the campfire, lost in thought, her book forgotten in her lap. The boys were at the nearby river, fishing for their dinner. Truthfully she could have gone to help them, they had always gone fishing together as kids, and she was just as good as they were. But she wanted to think, and to give the boys time together alone. They had all been through a lot the last few days and there was a certain companionship among men that did not involve a woman being present.

The flames danced in her eyes, a shifting of color and heat. She was worried about the future. Her mother had said that she had complete faith in Rosalie, but that was not the problem tonight. Rosalie knew her power, and her intellect, Crilla had not raised her to have self doubts. Though she had them anyway, especially where Jonaas was concerned. If she was honest with herself, much of the future scared her. At her core what she did not understand was why she had been chosen. She had so much responsibility ahead of her and centuries of life to live still. Which led to tonight's worrisome thoughts.

What was worrying her right now was The Weavers. The changes they had made were detestable, on that she agreed with her mother wholeheartedly. She also knew that power reigned within them, her abilities would eventually place her in a unique position to change things, for The Weavers, for herself, and for all of Innatraea. That weight was growing increasingly heavy upon her shoulders the further they got from home. But even that was not exactly the problem, she knew herself, and though she was scared, Rosalie also believed she was ready.

Time. That was the problem. For her mother, a former Weaver, and a woman who was hundreds of years old the changes were still recent. In truth though they had taken place decades ago. How much had those changes already ingrained themselves within The Weavers' beliefs? Was she going into an education, a fight, or a war? That was truly the problem, she was afraid of what her life would look like once she arrived on Sceotan. But at the same time, she was excited to become the woman she was meant to be. The most powerful Weaver on Innatraea. Worries aside there was no choice, her destiny hard as it was had been decided.

Then Rosalie heard voices from the trail towards the river, the boys were on their way back. She sighed and closed her book before setting it aside. She looked up as they entered the campsite, Edmond had four decent sized fish on a line, she did not know the specific species, as such things had never interested her. Jonaas took one look at her and his face grew concerned. "What's wrong?"

He had always been incredibly observant of her feelings, it was one of the many things she loved about him. "I am alright, just worrying about the future."

Jonaas sat by the fire. "I think we are all doing that. I don't even know what I'm doing yet to be honest."

Edmond sat down too, laying the fish in front of him, and drawing his knife. He looked at them both. "You two think too much." He gestured with the knife. "Look, do you remember what Crilla, and Gertrude used to say? It was an old world thing about the goddesses." He paused for a moment in thought, both she and Jonaas were looking at him startled, it was rare for Edmond to share such thoughts. "Let your feet follow your heart until you find your place of resurrection." He nodded to himself. "It means you're not supposed to overthink, just follow whatever your heart tells you to, until you find what you need. So look." He paused in gutting a fish and gestured with the knife again, looking at them both. "Rosalie your heart says go to Sceotan? Do it. Somewhere along the way you'll find what you're looking for."

Rosalie blinked and laughed. "Edmond, you giant oaf, you are right. I never imagined I would say that." She smiled at him and he laughed too.

Edmond looked at Jonaas. "What is your heart telling you to do?"

Jonaas looked into the campfire for a few moments, thinking, then met Edmond's eyes. "I think that I want to see more of Innatraea. Maybe I'll follow in Tavid's footsteps and go see Royal Seyla first. Shatranj is supposed to be very popular there."

Edmond nodded, while putting the first of the fish onto a stick for cooking. "Then it's decided. I'm going to Bethseda to join the Aedonian military, Rosalie will go to Sceotan to become a Weaver, and Jonaas will visit Royal Seyla. Somewhere each of us will find what we need."

Rosalie smiled, while looking at her two friends, she was going to miss them so much. Jonaas, and his heart, perhaps the kindest person she would ever meet, her first love, and the first man she had ever been with.

Gregarious Edmond and his bravado, yet underneath it all a caring man who just wanted the best for his friends. She took the skewered fish Edmond handed her, smiled at Jonaas, and held the stick over their campfire.

Jonaas got up to go check on Serra, who was happily tied to a nearby shrub. Rosalie watched him give the donkey an apple, and start brushing her. "You have always been so good to her."

He glanced over and smiled. "She's a good donkey, always has been."

Edmond held the remaining fish over the campfire. "Are you going to come cook your own food, farm boy?"

Jonaas laughed. "I'll be right there."

Rosalie smiled to herself, watching the two of them, then looked up at the Innatraea's three moons, bright in the sky. "Jonaas?" He looked at her. "The Three Sisters are bright tonight, bring your book too. I want to hear you read a few more times while we are all still together.

***

A few days later Jonaas put his hand up to shelter his eyes from the sun. "Is that smoke up ahead?" He glanced over as Edmond joined him, sheltering his eyes with a hand also.

"I think so, too much smoke for a campfire, plus it's too close to the road. What do you think, Rosalie?"

She stopped on Jonaas' other side and sheltered her eyes from the sun too. "Could be a small farm house or a wagon. There are supposed to be brigands that rob people on the king's highway, I hope no one is hurt."

Jonaas sighed, after days on the road, their first encounter with anyone else was going to be a bad one. He looked at his friends and smiled anyway, at least they were with him. "We should go take a look, someone may need help." He started walking, and clicked at Serra to get her moving, the cart wheels squeaked into motion.

They all crested a small rise and Jonaas looked ahead. The road went into a forest, and the smoke was coming from there. Which was bad, it didn't take much for a forest to catch fire this time of year, when all the brush was dry. Even if no one needed their help it was good they'd been here to see it. "Come on let's hurry it up, hopefully we can still make it in time to stop the fire from getting worse." He hurried his pace and clicked insistently at Serra.

His friends picked up their pace too, they'd all grown up near the woods, and knew how bad small blazes could get. Edmond in fact ran ahead, exuberant as always. "I'll beat you both there!"

Rosalie, walking quickly next to Jonas, rolled her eyes. "That boy is going to get himself killed someday. We will not always be here to watch after him."

Jonaas laughed. "I'm sure he'll be alright. He's brash, and gregarious, but he has a good heart and he's strong. He'll probably find a very responsible wife." Rosalie raised her brow at him and laughed too. They reached the bottom of the hill as Edmond disappeared into the forest.

Jonaas reached the tree line, with Rosalie right behind him. They didn't have to go very far. There was a burning merchant's wagon off the road shortly ahead. Edmond stood near it looking haunted, he looked up as they arrived. "They're already gone, someone did this to them."

Rosalie looked at the people laying around the wagon, one of them was a woman. She was face down in the mud, her dress was torn, and there was blood. Tears filled her eyes and she looked at Jonaas. "Why do people do this to one another Jonaas? Why?"

He hugged her gently. "I don't know, but we can give their souls peace at least." He stepped away and looked around. "Rosalie put the fire out. Edmond you and I will bury them off the road, near the trees. Hopefully there's peace in that." His friends nodded.

***

Barth watched the three young travelers reach the wagon, from his hiding spot in the trees. He'd been checking the road for patrols when he saw them coming, it was always a good idea to know what was happening around your band. Then he saw the two boys start dragging the bodies away to bury them and laughed to himself, what fools. Why waste your time on the dead? He and his men had already had their fun, and taken what valuables the wagon had, anything more was just a waste of time. The young girl with them was very pretty, why did the two boys leave her alone like that? Maybe he'd come back with his men and wait for an opportunity, it didn't seem like this lot had any idea how things worked in the real world.

Then he got the shock of his life. The young girl looked at the flaming wagon, twirled her hands a little bit, and fire went out. She was a Weaver, which explained why they'd left her alone. But she was still young, how much experience did she have? Maybe if they knocked her out fast, or arrowed her, she'd drop before being able to weave anything.

Barth rubbed his chin in thought, were those boys bound to her? He'd heard about that a while back. How good was the one with his nice looking sword? How much was that nice looking sword worth? He slunk away to get his men before the three started moving again, that way they could follow them or set up an ambush ahead. Maybe there'd be a good opportunity.

Chapter Twelve:
A Weaver's Strength

They made good time over the next few days. One evening they made camp in a clearing beside a river. The surrounding woods were thick, and they built their campfire as far from the trees as they could to avoid setting the trees on fire.

Rosalie watched Jonaas curry Serra. He paused for a moment, took the rough stone pendant from around his neck, and stuffed it in his pocket. Rosalie found that curious. "Why not wear it?"

Jonaas looked at her with sad eyes. "I've tried wearing it a few times after you put it around my neck. But I'm not ready to face what it means yet; it feels too heavy."

Edmond looked up from his spot by the campfire. He had insisted upon lighting it tonight, even though Rosalie could have lit it with just a thought. "Heavy? It is just a necklace."

Jonaas joined them by the fire. "Yes, but it represents a people I don't know, and my mother who was attacked then died giving birth to me. It's heavy."

Rosalie put her arm around Jonaas's shoulder and drew him closer.

Edmond, meanwhile, stared into the campfire thoughtfully.

"I understand," Edmond said quietly. "Not knowing who you are and where you come from is hard."

Rosalie nodded. "Truthfully, I do not know where I came from either. You know that Crilla found me in a basket, floating on the river. What you don't know is that she tried hard to find out where I came from but never did." She opened her free hand, made a few small, different colored glow orbs, and floated them around in front of the here of them. "I have had a good life though. I love where I grew up, and I have friends who I love. I do not think where we come from decides who we are, we do that for ourselves."

She closed her hand, and the glow orbs vanished. She sat up and took both the boys' hands. "We decide who we are, and we come from Aliselle Falls, together." The boys nodded their agreement.

Suddenly an arrow flew past Rosalie's head, missing by a very narrow margin, before hitting a tree near Serra. A group of men burst out of the trees, screaming and wielding clubs, axes, and knives. Edmond stood and drew his sword. Jonaas only had his hunting knife, but he drew it and stood anyway, trying to put himself between Rosalie and the nearest of the marauding men.

Rosalie could not tell exactly how many there were, or the movements of each, because it was getting dark, and the assault was chaotic. But Edmond was skillfully holding off some of the knife-wielders with his sword, so Rosalie was much more worried about Jonaas. He was moving toward two men with wicked-looking clubs, trying to fend them off with his hunting knife. They both swung at him, but he managed to dodge the blows and stuck his knife into one man's side. When the man grunted in pain, instead of pushing his advantage Jonaas froze for a moment. He had never hurt anyone before; her gentle farm boy just did not have violence in him.

The other man took advantage of Jonaas's hesitation and swung at his head. The blow would have killed Jonaas if Rosalie's weaves of air had not stopped the club midair. She advanced on the two men, shouting in rage, "You do not touch him!" One of the men she skewered with a small spear of flame. The other one watched in shock, but quickly recovered and tried to grab for Jonaas. But he could not move faster than her weaves; none of them could. She swept his legs with a lasso of fire, then dragged him along the ground into other men nearby, creating a pile of burning, chaotic, flailing limbs, and shouting. Someone yelled, "The Weaver is still up! Get her fast or use one of the boys as a hostage!"

She strode to where most of them were, fiery rope-like lashes sweeping the air ahead of her, knocking them down like wood, and burning them as she advanced, screaming, "How dare you!" One of the marauders cut Edmond on his side as he was busy blocking another one's jab.

Hearing Edmond cry out in pain, Rosalie pulled the man away in a cord of fire that engulfed him.

Something struck her shoulder. She cried out in pain and faltered, but Jonaas was there, and he wrapped his arm around her supportively. She looked around quickly. There were at least a dozen still. She was tired, and it was getting darker. She had to end this now.

Stepping back from Jonaas's supporting arm, Rosalie created a large blood-red glow orb above the campsite. The glow illuminated everything in a horrible visage of writhing blood and fire. Its menacing look added to the whirling lashes of flame that still burned all those they touched. "Leave now and live!"

The invaders – what was left of them – fled in terror. And she thanked the goddesses that they did because she was so tired.

Rosalie blacked out and collapsed into Jonaas' arms.

***

Barth watched his bowman, Clyde draw back his bow, aiming the arrow at the pretty little Weaver. After he shot her, their friends would pounce on the two boys. Then they would take her, the sword, and whatever else of value these kids had. Young innocents were easy prey to the likes of himself and his men. He did love a good ambush, especially when it was followed by murder, thievery, and a good bit of fun too.

Then he heard a horrible, rumbling growl to their side. He turned and beheld the most horrifying thing he'd ever seen: a dark, shadowy wolf, bigger than a horse, with flaming yellow eyes. Clyde's shot went wide, as the thing snapped the man's neck with one bite. It turned to Barth, its huge teeth dripping blood and chunks of meat, and growled again.

Barth screamed and ran, heedless of direction, not pausing even to warn his men. He could hear the thumping of the monster's huge feet behind him, like death itself chasing him through the woods. Feeling its presence, he looked up to see the massive, bloody maw descending upon him. The sounds of his own screams, and the snapping of his neck, were the last things he heard.

***

A few evenings later, Jonaas was sitting near Rosalie who was lying on her blankets in their new campsite. Since the attack, they had walked as far as they could, while she slept in the cart, until they found a new campsite with a better view of the surrounding landscape. This way they would see any attackers long before they arrived.

Rosalie had been in a deep sleep the entire time. But her breathing was calm and undisturbed, and as Jonaas sat there stroking her hair, he had time to think back on the fight at their last campsite. He had never seen Rosalie like that before. Enraged, out of control, even more powerful than usual. It was a side of her that impressed him, though he hoped he would never have to see it again.

Her eyes fluttered open, and she looked at him. "Why are you staring at me?"

Jonaas smiled. "You've been asleep for so long. I'm just happy to see your beautiful eyes again."

Rosalie shot upright. "Edmond was cut in the attack! Is he alright?" She looked around the campsite frantically until she spotted him by the campfire, changing the bandages around his middle. "You are alright, thank the goddesses! Come here, let me heal that for you."

Edmond didn't move. "I'm alright. The cut wasn't deep, a little bandaging and I should be fine."

She arched her eyebrow at him.

Edmond laughed and gestured with his hands before coming to sit by them. "Peace! You can heal me."

After Edmond removed his bandages, Rosalie laid her hands on his side. His wound healed in seconds leaving no sign that he had ever been wounded. He flexed his arm and stretched his side, laughing. "Good as new, thank you! That power of yours never ceases to amaze me. I think I'll miss that more than you!"

She punched him in the shoulder, and he laughed again. But he and Jonaas grew concerned when she grunted in pain and rotated her left shoulder gently.

She of course noticed and spoke before either of them could ask. "I am alright, I must have slept on it wrong." Edmond retreated to his spot near the campfire without a word and turned over the rabbits he had been roasting.

Rosalie wrapped her arms around her knees and laid her head down.

It took Jonaas a moment to realize that she was crying softly. He laid a hand on her shoulder. "What's wrong? We're all alive thanks to you."

She looked up with eyes that were red and swimming with tears. "Jonaas, I killed someone!"

He wasn't sure what to say. Without her they'd all be dead. But she was right, and he didn't know how to help her with that burden.

Thankfully, Edmond spoke up. "Yes, you did."

Rosalie looked at him, her eyes questioning. He met her gaze. "Look. Life is hard for everyone. Without you doing what you did those men would have killed us, raped you, and sold all our things at the nearest town."

She put her head down and sobbed, Jonaas squeezed her shoulder. "We're not at home anymore, Innatraea isn't as kind as we're all used to.

Rosalie?"

She looked up at Jonaas again.

"Edmond is right. I know you didn't want to do that, and I'm sorry you had to, but the alternative was all of us dead rather than them." He held out his arms and she laid on his lap, so he could hold her. "I have the feeling Weavers have a lot of such decisions in their lives."

Rosalie stared into the flickering campfire, her eyes sensitive and tired. "I do not want them. I do not know if I am strong enough, Jonaas. Not for that."

He hugged her tighter. "You're stronger than you think. We all know it."

Rosalie closed her eyes and snuggled against him, closing her eyes.

"Goddess, I hated having to do that, but I know both of you are right."

***

Before long, Rosalie had drifted off to sleep. This time her sleep was fitful, and Jonaas imagined she must be dreaming of the bloody battle two days before. He gently stroked her hair, hoping to keep her asleep. She needed it.

"Do you remember hearing a wolf out in the woods?" Jonaas asked Edmond. "During the fight with those men?"

"A wolf? I didn't hear anything like that, but I was pretty busy," Edmond said. He poked the rabbits roasting over the fire. "I think dinner is ready."

Jonaas gently shook Rosalie's shoulder, waking her again. "The meat is cooked, and you need to eat."

She got up and went over to the campfire. Watching her go, Jonaas worried about her fragile emotional state after killing a man for the first time. All he could do was keep an eye on her and be there for her if the memory shook her again.

Meanwhile, he had something else to worry about, and that was a creature whose size and strength he could only guess by its horrible growl. Hopefully, they would never come face to face with it.

Chapter Thirteen:
Grief

"Grief can swallow even the strongest Innatraean's heart. A Weaver can never afford such weakness."
-Crilla Sharone

The following few days passed without incident. The three travelers made their way along the river or occasional dirt road mostly in silence, lost in their individual thoughts. The burning wagon and the poor merchant's family especially consumed Edmond's thoughts. And those horrible, murderous men! Rosalie, he knew, had taken those events harder than even himself or Jonaas. The King's Highway was so much different from home. Out here in the wild, danger seemed to await them behind every tree and rock. Edmond's training had made him skilled at fighting, but his lessons had been limited to swordplay and hand-to-hand combat, not watching for danger everywhere and fending off ambushes from the shadows.

He knew the ambush a few days ago had rattled Rosalie and Jonaas as well. Their silence made that obvious. Maybe it was time to get his friends talking again.

He looked over at Rosalie who was using her power to clean the campsite they had set up the night before. Their things hovered into the cart, the fire went out, the water jugs dipped into the nearby creek on their own, and their latrine covered itself in fresh loam.

"Crilla said most Weavers don't use their powers for menial tasks," Edmond commented. "She said they're not that strong."

Rosalie raised her eyebrow at him. "I am stronger than I used to be Whenever a Weaver pushes themselves like I did, and survives, they get stronger."

"Edmond and I could have done all that cleaning," Jonaas said. "Breakfast would have been nice too."

"One does not become a master of their craft by skipping the fundamentals. Also, I need to use my newfound strength." She paused thoughtfully. "I also need to learn how to deal with what happened."

"How about floating some food over here before we start walking?" Edmond said.

Rosalie smiled, and an apple, a chunk of cheese, and a hunk of bread came flying in Edmond's direction. He had to move quickly to catch them all. "Your breakfast, Ser Carlon."

Jonaas laughed but not for long, as he too found himself trying to catch his food out of the air. Edmond smiled with satisfaction. It was good to see his friends enjoying a light moment again.

"Jonaas, you should come join the Aedonian lists after Royal Seyla," Edmond said. You're sharp and capable; you'll advance quickly. If you could apply your mastery of Shatranj to battle, you'd be a general."

Jonaas lifted his book *Tavid the Traveler* out of his shoulder bag and riffled through the pages. "I'm not sure. Part of me just wants to go home after that. I still don't feel like I belong there, not after what I learned." He touched the pocket where he kept that rough stone pendant now. "So, I plan to keep traveling for a while. Where I belong is still out there somewhere."

Edmond sighed. He had expected as much from his friend, though he'd hoped otherwise. He understood that Jonaas needed to keep looking. "I understand. I hope you find what you need out there."

"I do not much like the idea of you traveling alone for so long, you are not made the same as us," Rosalie told Jonaas. "But I understand your reasoning. Is that truly what you wish to do?"

Jonaas nodded. "Yes. Traveling seems like the right thing for me to do. I'm not sure where I belong yet, but I'll find out. I won't be alone anyway; Serra will be with me." He laughed and Edmond couldn't hope but join in. Rosalie just raised her eyebrow at the both of them.

***

Later that evening, Rosalie wiggled her finger and their campfire burst into flame again. The finger wiggling was not necessary, but it helped when she was tired. She also conjured a glow orb so she could see better.

Innatrae's moons, the Three Sisters, were out, but they and the fire only provided so much light.

Jonaas and Edmond were rolled up in their cloaks, asleep. Boys ran around exuberantly all day, then collapsed into a stupor when there was nothing important to do like eating or discussing plans, she observed to herself. Well then, it was time to relax and read a little. She needed the distraction, and truthfully, the quiet too. She had not understood how hard becoming a Weaver was going to be out in Innatraea, away from home.

Things were so different – and so much worse – out here in the wilds.

She opened her satchel, meaning to read one of her two favorite books that her mother had sent with her. A letter fell out with them, and Rosalie picked it up. It was addressed to "Sister Taia", one of her mother's oldest friends. Rosalie used a small thread of fire to make the wax seal let go of the paper and opened it. The beginning of the long letter was about her:

"Rosalie is my legacy. I have raised her since she was a small child. Her skills, use of intellect, and logic are unparalleled among those of similar age. She is, however, very headstrong and liable to get herself into trouble..."

She smiled and held the letter against her heart. How she wished either of the two boys was going with her! Looking at them, lost in their dreams, she sighed. Being on her own was going to be a challenge. Yet Crilla believed in her, and this was her path.

She melted the wax seal again and placed the letter aside. There were still a few things left in her satchel, and she decided to examine them all in case something else was there that her mother hadn't told her about.

The next thing she took out was a few coin pouches filled to the top.

More than enough for a few days at an inn, meals, and a ship to reach Sceotan from Haversfjord once they got there. She was about to investigate the royal scripts her mother had packed when she felt heat on her chest. It seemed to emanate from her mother's ring which hung there on its cord. Fear crept into her heart, and she yanked the chain out of her bodice to look. The ring glowed. The small threads that made a pattern around it were undulating in a strange current as if they were alive. Panic began to creep in: a Weaver's ring was not supposed to reshape itself for its legacy unless its Weaver was dead. She started crying. The events at home just before they left, their encounters on the road, the man falling dead from her flames, and now the possibility that her mother was gone all piled onto her like a mountain.

The only way to be sure was to put the ring on her own finger, even though her heart recoiled at the idea. She hesitated, lost in trepidation and sorrow. Finally, ever so slowly, she slipped the ring on. It burned brighter and it hurt, but it also fit perfectly. Its small, glowing threads rearranged themselves into a new pattern and cooled, settling onto her finger as though the ring had always belonged to her and her alone.

Something inside of her broke like a dam in a great storm. That storm became a real thing, a cyclone, surrounding their campsite. Rosalie stood, fists clenched at her side, weeping, screaming, and unaware of what was happening. The cyclone uprooted trees, moved rocks, and sent chunks of dirt and plants into the air. Only the campsite remained calm in the cyclone's eye, as the winds of her rage and sadness savaged the forest around them. The keening wind sounded like a living thing, expressing Rosalie's grief in the only way it could – by destroying everything in its path.

Inside that keening mass glow orbs, bright but distorted in shape, color and size, danced and twisted within the whirling storm, like caricatures of its destructive power. She did not see Jonaas and Edmond wake up, did not see Edmond run to hold onto Serra as Jonaas came to her. Her eyes crackled with lightning, the rage and sorrow inside her hungered for release. But then there was something else. Something between her and Jonaas, between his feeble voice and the mass of her whirling wrath and sadness.

Rosalie felt a doorway open, though it was not really a doorway at all. Was it real? Where did it lead to? Had she seen this doorway before? She felt as though she had, same as the farm field had before.

A sense of calm settled over her. It seemed to come from somewhere outside her yet from within her as well. The storm died, and she fell into Jonaas' waiting arms. He pulled her close without saying a word, and the world faded.

CHAPTER FOURTEEN: RESURRECTION

"Let your feet follow your heart until you find your place of resurrection."
-Old World Goddess Saying

Jonaas looked up from the rabbits he was roasting on a spit over the campfire. Edmond was just returning after feeding and grooming Serra for him. "How is my girl?" Jonaas asked.

"Good. Happy." Edmond smiled. "Didn't miss you a bit." Jonaas smirked, but the smile quickly faded.

Edmond saw the worry on his face. "How's Rosalie?" Jonaas sighed. "The same."

Rosalie lay sleeping nearby. It had been a few days since she collapsed in Jonaas's arms, and she still hadn't awakened. He hoped she would wake up soon, not so much because they were losing precious travel time, but because he was deeply concerned about her. Her tirade a few days ago after putting on Crilla's ring had shaken him deeply. For years, he had known Rosalie as well as anyone could, yet he realized he still knew very little about the Weaver part of her. Was it normal for a Weaver to have these events so close together? Would she lose weight from not eating?

How long could she stay unconscious? He wondered if he and Edmond should take her back home to Crilla. Most of all, he wondered why she was wearing Crilla's ring. He was anxious, scared, and had no idea what to do about any of it.

One of her hands flexed, as if trying to grab something in her sleep. It was the first movement Jonaas had seen since she fell into this deep sleep.

As if reading his thoughts, Edmond said, "That whole thing a few days ago – it was terrifying. How strong do you think she is now?"

"I honestly don't know. I never saw Crilla do anything like that. I never even heard of a Weaver doing anything like that."

"I'm just glad we were with her when it happened."

"How long do you think these blackouts last?" Jonaas asked. "We won't be with her forever. It scares me."

Edmond didn't answer but nodded toward Rosalie. Jonaas looked and saw she was stirring. First her arms then her mouth began to move. In a dry voice she called, "Jonaas?"

Elated, Jonaas leaned over and took her hand. "I'm here, Rosalie, you're safe."

Her eyes opened and she slowly sat up.

"I feel like I have been sleeping for days." She looked around the neat little campsite. "Where are we? Did you boys keep walking while I was asleep? How far did we go? How long have I been asleep?" Running her hands through her hair, she caught sight of Crilla's ring on her finger. "Oh no, no! How? Oh, Crilla!"

Tears filled her eyes. Jonaas held her in his arms and let her cry on his chest.

"What happened?" Edmond asked. "What about Crilla?"

Rosalie held up the hand with the ring. " She is dead. Her ring. I would not be able to wear it otherwise. What has happened back home?"

"We don't know," Jonaas said. "We can go back together if you want to. Gertrude may need me too."

"No," Edmond said before Rosalie could answer. Jonaas looked at him, angry, but Edmond waved him off. "We've all lost people. I wish as much as you that we knew what happened. But we have to press on. I lost my grandmother; Jonaas, you basically lost your mother. I know you loved Crilla, Rosalie – we all did – but we have to follow our hearts still. It's what they all would have wanted for us."

Rosalie pulled away from Jonaas. Tears still ran down her cheeks, but something had changed. Behind the grief, a fierce, deep shine showed through in her eyes. Jonaas had never seen such a resolute expression on her face. It was marvelous.

"You are right, we all have to go on." She held the ring up and looked at it. "I will accomplish everything my mother and I ever wanted. I am the Legacy of Crilla Sharone, and I will triumph."

She looked around, as if startled at her own certainty, then her eyes settled upon the rabbits cooking over the campfire. She grabbed one and went to work on it with the will of a starving person. The young men grinned, unused to seeing Rosalie act so primal. This earned them a glare between bites of rabbit.

From the road came the sounds of horses, and a man yelled, "Ho the camp."

Edmond stood and sheathed his sword which he'd been sharpening. "Sounds like soldiers," he said. "I've got this." To Jonaas, he added, "Make sure she stays here until I know what's going on." This earned him another glare from Rosalie, but he didn't seem to notice as he walked toward the road.

***

At the road Edmond saw nearly a dozen soldiers on horseback, their white tabards and chainmail gleaming in the sun. He could tell they were Aedonian soldiers by the House D'Arganse emblem on their chest.

Everyone knew D'Arganse was the ruling house of Aedonia. Thankfully, there were no Jhorian forces with them. If so, they might be after Rosealie.

The soldier nearest to the camp bore the mark of a sergeant at arms on his tabard. Edmond nodded respectfully to him. "Ser, how can we help you?"

The man nodded in return. "Where are you three headed?"

"We're headed up to Bethseda. I plan on signing the lists, and my two friends are coming with me."

The man thought for a moment then nodded. "There have been reports of attacks on the road lately. We've been sent to patrol and investigate. Be careful and see that you get a move on soon."

Edmond nodded. "We will Ser. Thank you for your diligence."

The man eyed Edmond's sword momentarily before snapping his reins and riding back to the other soldiers. Soon they were all trotting down the road again. Edmond waited until they were gone then went back to his friends.

"It was Aedonian soldiers, not Jhorians," he told them. "They said there's been reports of travelers being attacked. They're patrolling the road to investigate."

Rosalie looked thoughtful. "Do you think it is those men who attacked us?"

"Probably. But just in case, we should get moving and be more careful where we camp. I think we will reach the road to Haversfjord today."

Jonaas said to Rosalie, "It's probably best that you don't use Weaving for a while, and also put the ring away. We don't know who's out there, and it would be bad if any soldiers – or worse, Jhorian Crows –figured out you're a Weaver."

Rosalie sighed and stood up, dusting off her dress. "Yes, I think that you are both right. But I cannot take off Crilla's ring. It is still attuning itself to me." She looked around the camp. "You boys can take care of this, I am going to say hi to Serra."

Edmond laughed, calling after her, "You know that means your dress will get dirty now! No more Weaving to clean it."

***

99

That night as Rosalie and Edmond slept, Jonaas stood a short ways from their campsite looking at The Three Sisters, Innatraea's moons, high in the night sky. He was recalling Gertrude's words as she handed him the rough stone pendant on its leather cord: *"This belonged to your mother."* He could still feel his confusion. What did she mean by 'your mother' he had wondered. Gertrude was his mother.

"She didn't make it through your birth, and I promised her I'd tell you the truth one day. Your mother was Rinowhn; her name was Chaya.

Jonathan and I found her on the road after she'd been attacked, and we took care of her." So the woman buried under the apple trees was his mother. What did that make him, besides the son of a horrible tragedy?

His hand closed around the rough stone pendant in his pocket. How was he supposed to face that part of himself?

Rosalie's arms wrapped around him from behind. "Why are you not asleep?" she whispered. When he did not respond, she came around to look at him. "Jonaas, what is wrong?"

"I'm alright. Just remembering." He wiped his eyes and tried to smile.

Who am I, Rosalie? What kind of man is born that way?"

She met his eyes. Love, compassion, and anger were all there in those beautiful, gleaming pools of green. Her hand went around his jaw, and she pulled his face toward hers, her eyes deep and intense. "No. You are the man that I love, a kind, intelligent, loyal, and brave friend. Your mother's tragedy, though beyond sad, is not you. Do you hear me Jonaas? Your birth does not define your destiny."

Jonaas smiled for real this time. He embraced her, laying his head on her shoulder. "I know you're right, it's just still so new for me. I need to know who I am, Rosalie."

She stroked his hair gently. "I know somewhere out there you will find what you need, just stay safe."

He took her hand on his, noticing her ring, it looked different, still made of the familiar colorful patterned strands but their shape had changed. "Your ring has changed, I didn't know they could do that."

She smiled sadly, looking at it too. "It will keep doing so throughout my life, as I change, it will too." Her voice choked. "Though a piece of my mother will always be there."

"I'm sorry, you've been through so much too."

She sighed and kissed his forehead. "We have all been through a lot, Jonaas. It is alright to seek comfort when you need it. We are friends and I love you."

Jonaas remembered Rosalie's love for Innatraea's Great Trees and her desire to see them. They were ancient giant trees that held sacred significance to those who followed The Three Sisters, but there weren't any near Aliselle Falls where they'd grown up. "While you were asleep, Edmond and I spotted what we think is The Shepherd King to the north," he said. "The Great Tree you told us once belonged to Dryad Daphne – we could go out of our way for a few days and see it if you want to."

Rosalie laid her forehead against his and closed her eyes, sighing. "I would love to, Jonaas, you know I would. But we are out in Aedonia now, and the chances of running into Jhorian Crows is too high. I have to reach Haversfjord and get on a ship as soon as possible. That is how I will stay safe."

Jonaas sighed, holding her close. She was right and he knew it. He closed his eyes, and they held each other for a while longer.

Chapter Fifteen:
The Peddler's Respite

"An inn's common room is one of the few places commoners, soldiers, merchants, knights, and nobles of all lands can meet amicably; but you must always practice care."
– Tavid the Traveler

Edmond looked down the road at the river town of Haversfjord in the distance. He had never seen a town so big. Great ships crowded its large harbor or moved along the massive Victory River which came from the north, and flowed onwards southwest. The town itself sprawled out like a crowded, disorganized mess. Edmond sighed. Normally he would have been excited at such an amazing new place, but soon everything would change. Rosalie would be headed to Sceotan (hopefully before there was any trouble; there would probably be danger for her in this town), Edmond would head north to Bethseda, and Jonaas would apparently be going south to Royal Seyla. Haversfjord represented a sad parting of ways for the three friends, much like the diverging rivers that ran past it.

Jonaas walked up beside him guiding Serra and their cart. He scratched the donkey's ears and surveyed the town too.

"Everything will change now, " Edmond said, speaking both their thoughts aloud.

Jonaas nodded. "I'm excited to see Innatraea, and happy for you both to have found your paths. But I'll miss you and Rosalie a lot."

From behind them came Rosalie's voice. "Are you both ready for this?"

"I am, even though it will be hard," Jonaas told her. "Rosalie, I hve

read about Haversfjord in Tavid the Traveler. There's a Jhorian temple here. You should stay inside whatever inn we choose, to be safe."

Rosalie stopped beside Jonaas. For a moment she looked like she would argue with him. But then her eyes grew soft, and she nodded.

Edmond said, "Do you think we'll see each other again?"

"I think so," Rosalie said. "Once I have completed my training I will be a Weaver, then I can go anywhere I want to. Jonaas will probably still be wandering around somewhere." She glanced at him, a twinkle in her eyes.

Jonaas grinned. "Maybe I'll even be in Sceotan by then. Who knows?"

A merchant wagon rolled by, and the wagon driver yelled at them to get a move on or get off the road. Rosalie twitched her little finger – the boys had learned to notice such things growing up around her – and one of the wagon's wheels groaned ominously. The man looked down, worried, and pulled off the road.

"Come on, let us go find an inn," Rosalie said, starting in the direction of the town. "I plan to bathe and sleep in a bed tonight."

Edmond laughed and started after her. "Come on Jonaas, let's find a good inn before she shoves us into some fancy lady's gossip parlor!"

The boys caught up to Rosalie just outside the town gates. Guards watched them enter, but didn't say anything. Rosalie pointed at an inn across the way. A woman happily carrying a basket of feathers was displayed on the sign. The lettering beneath read, The Lady's Feather.

Edmond rolled his eyes. "No way!" He pointed farther down the street to another inn, The Boar's Redoubt. "How about that one?"

Rosalie started to protest, but Jonaas spoke first. "I'll make this easy on both of you." He pointed at a third inn across the way. The sign out front read The Peddler's Respite. "That one has a stable." He headed that way, clicking at Serra to keep her moving, before either of them could reply.

***

Later that evening, Jonaas came down the stairs to the inn's common room, feeling refreshed after a long bath. It did feel good to be clean again, though it had cost extra to have access to the men's bathing chambers.

The common room had been nearly empty when they arrived earlier, but the evening had brought more travelers looking for a meal and a safe place to stay overnight. Jonaas understood why when he smelled food and heard his belly rumble.

He looked around the common room and found Edmond already

sitting at a table, ale and food in front of him. Jonaas joined him.

"Is that mutton?" Jonaas asked.

Edmond shoveled food into his mouth and gulped his ale. "Yes, and it's very good!"

Jonaas ordered for himself. When the serving girl brought his meal he threw in a few extra coppers for her.

"You're way too nice to everyone," Edmond said after the girl left.

Keep doing that and you'll be broke in no time."

Jonaas took a bite of mutton and looked around the room. "I think I'll be just fine. Look over there."

He nodded toward a table by one of the windows, where a well-dressed nobleman or knight was seated with a glass of wine, staring at a Shatranj board.

Edmond scoffed. "Good luck!" They knocked their tankards together and drank.

Rosalie appeared at the stairs, looking fresh and clean and beautiful as always. Jonaas lifted his tankard and smiled at her as she joined them at the table. She met his eyes and smiled coyly, but quickly looked away to scan the inn's common room.

"I do believe that I hate traveling," she said. She looked at their food and added, "I hope there is something else to eat and drink here."

Jonaas waved the serving girl over and pointed at Rosalie. He got up. "I'll be back in a bit."

He went over to the table where he'd seen the man with the Shatranj board earlier.

"Excuse me Ser, care for a game?"

The man looked at him skeptically. "Are you a farmer lad? Shatranj is a gentleman's game."

Jonaas smiled and removed the last silver mark from his pouch. "A wager then?"

The man looked him over again and placed a gold mark near the board before setting up the pieces. "Why not? I'm in a good mood today. Let's see what you have, lad. My name is Ser Kehlmar."

Jonaas took the other chair and shook the man's hand. "Jonaas Al'Shane, farmer."

*

Magnus Kehlmar looked across the board at this farm boy, Jonaas, while considering his next move. They'd been playing for a while, and he had begun to realize just how marvelous a player the boy was. A small group, including the boy's friends, had gathered around the table to watch. Some were making wagers of their own.

Magnus had to admit he'd been sandbagged. What he thought would be an easy silver had quickly turned into him fending for his gold mark like a drowning man trying to keep his head above water. Most people had a particular strategy in Shatranj; to figure out an opponent's strategy was to defeat that opponent. The phase of the game in which this became clear said a lot about a player's strength. This boy, however, flowed from one strategy to another as easily as breathing. It was a marvel to watch, though not as enjoyable to experience with one's money at stake.

Magnus thought back to the moment his losing had become a certainty. The farm boy had been forming The King's Quarter. He knew that strategy, and had been setting up to defeat it, when within a few moves it faded, and Jonaas' pieces fell into the elephant's charge. Most of the game had gone like that.

Magnus sighed, making his mind up and placing his soldier down.

The farm boy looked up at him and smiled, moving a ruhk. "Fahz nihaya." His two friends laughed and smiled too, and money exchanged hands here and there throughout the small crowd.

The game was over. Magnus blinked and scanned the board. He shook off a flash of anger and laughed, shoving the gold mark across the table toward his victorious opponent. "Where did you learn to play like that?"

Jonaas smiled and picked up the mark. "My father taught me, though where he learned I don't know, and to be honest, I've been beating him for years now." A flicker of sadness crossed the boy's face. "Thank you for the game, Ser Kehlmar, you're an excellent player."

Magnus laughed again. "I thought so as well until today! I'll be here for a few days before heading to Royal Seyla. If you want to play again, look for me."

"Royal Seyla?" Jonaas said. "I was planning on heading there too.

Have you been there before?"

Magnus regarded the boy across the table. He'd forgotten just how young his opponent actually was, and that he was a farmer of all things.

The boy had probably never been anywhere. "I have. It's a nice place, a beautiful city and great food, though spicy. The women are also something to behold, and their Companions are known all over Innatraea. There's an annual Shatranj tournament in Kinrai, the capital, a few months from now. That's where I'm headed, and you're welcome to join me."

The boy smiled. "That sounds like an excellent idea. Thank you."

Chapter Sixteen: Our Last Days

"Never despair your last days among friends, for an Innatraean's soul does not recognize that distance."
– Tavid the Traveler

That night, Jonaas stopped outside Rosalie's door and lifted his hand to knock, but he couldn't do it. For a few moments he stayed there in front of the door, debating whether to go through with this. All day he had been wanting a heart-to-heart with her. In a few days they would split up and go their separate ways; after that he might not see Rosalie again for a long time, if ever. He wanted her so badly he could feel it in his body as he stood outside her door. But she was going to be a Weaver, and a good one.

Rosalie had always been the best of the three friends, and Jonaas couldn't bring himself to jeopardize that. There was also Crilla to think about; what had happened to her? Was Rosalie alright? He could just ask her...

Sighing, he dropped his hand and walked away, suddenly needing some fresh air.

Outside, he headed for the harbor to watch the ships. He'd never actually seen a sailing ship before, and he thought it could be interesting. He stopped at a nice spot under a large tree and leaned against the railing, watching the sailors on the docked boats finishing their work for the day. He was still thinking about his friends and couldn't help remembering the closing words of his favorite book by Tavid the Traveler. Friends may split apart over long distances, Tavid wrote, but their souls didn't recognize that. Jonaas truly hoped this was true.

He shook himself and looked back at the working sailors, mostly as a distraction from those thoughts. Sailing work looked hard. Everything they were doing required a strong body, from moving casks to winding heavy ropes and even moving sails around. He also noticed how different many of the sailors looked. He couldn't name where they were all from, though he knew a few from reading Tavid's book. The bare-chested, tan, or dark-skinned and tattooed sailors were Am'ayim. The ones with the cloth-wrapped hats were Tursi. He was also pretty sure the tall, light-skinned sailors were Nordrian. Trade towns like Haversfjord must have seen people from all over Innatraea, and Jonaas couldn't wait to see all these different places and people himself. He felt lighter and a bit happier just thinking about it.

A man leaned on the railing near him, and Jonaas looked over. He was tall and older-looking, with gray hair, a gray beard, and wise blue eyes. He wore chainmail and a sword at his side. "Hello there lad, enjoying the evening?" the man asked.

Jonaas nodded and smiled. "I am. This is my first time in such a large town."

The man chuckled. "Well, that answers my question. For a moment I thought I knew you from somewhere, even though you're much too young." He offered Jonaas his hand and they shook. "I'm the local Reeve, Archibald Stallwood."

"Jonaas Al'Shane. I was a farmer. My friends and I just arrived recently. We're from Aliselle Falls. I must have one of those familiar faces, because this is my first time out of my hometown."

"It's good to meet you lad. Where are you headed?"

"I'll be going to Kinrai, in Royal Seyla, first. After that, I'm not sure." "Traveling, eh? My one piece of advice is not to tell people where you're from, or that it's your first time out in the world. And try not to look so much like an innocent farm boy. Innatraea can be an unfriendly place for the innocent."

Jonaas nodded. "I'll consider that, thank you Reeve Stallwood" "Have a good evening and stay safe on your travels." The man nodded to Jonaas and headed on his way.

Jonaas stayed a while longer, watching the sailors and thinking. He wanted to go back to Rosalie, but there was a weight between them. He could feel it. She was so much stronger now, and on her way to greatness, while he was still just a farmer. Then there was Crilla. He recalled Rosalie's screams and the forest being destroyed. It had been terrifying. How was he supposed to be there for his friend now? He didn't like the thought, but maybe it was better they would be separating soon.

***

The next morning, Rosalie went down to the docks accompanied by

Jonaas and Edmond. At dockside, she closed her eyes and thought of Crilla. Knowing what must have happened to her mother made her want to cry. But her mother would want her to go on, so she opened her eyes, wiped them with the back of her hand, and surveilled the ship she had chosen for her journey. It was long and sleek for a cargo ship, with golden decorations and a figurehead shaped like a roaring lion leaping out of ocean waves. The ship's flag featured two golden hands holding a brown ship emblazoned on a white background. It was an Am'ayim vessel judging by the tan- or dark-skinned sailors working on her. Rosalie thought back to the time when Crilla instructed her on such things. "The best way to travel is with the Am'ayim," Crilla had advised. "Their ships are faster, their sailors more skilled, and if you demand ka'u malihini taumatau, or "guest right," during negotiations they will be more honest than others."

"Please wait here for me, I can handle this," she told Jonaas and Edmond before heading over to the gangplank. They looked skeptical but stayed put.

Up on the deck, she felt the ship move under her feet with the river. It was a feeling she hadn't experienced before, and she found it disconcerting. But now was no time to second guess herself.

A burly Am'ayim sailor standing next to the gangplank looked her up and down and grinned. He was bare-chested, with dark skin and tattoos. His hair was braided in a long series of small knots, almost like a climbing rope. In a deep but amused voice, he said, "How wi can help yuh likkle missy?"

Rosalie had to listen closely to understand his speech. It was basically Innatraea's common tongue, but heavily accented and with an odd sentence structure. She nodded politely. As annoying as the man eyeing her was, Crilla had taught her that this was normal and no reason to stop negotiations. "I wish to secure passage to Sceotan."

The uncouth sailor whistled through a gap in his teeth and spat into the water. "Dat a waan expensive trip likkle missy."

Again it took her a moment but not as long this time. Rosalie sighed and raised her hand. "My name is Rosalie, not lil' missy. You will address me as such while I am aboard your vessel." She pointed at the water where he had spat. "You will also not do that again in my presence. I am no plebeian."

The man blinked. "Mi nuh know who yuh tink yuh be..."

Another man stepped up and placed a hand on his shoulder. "Mi ago be handle di young lady, tank yuh Absai."

Rosalie looked at the newcomer. He was an older Am'ayim, though lighter-skinned and displaying a more pleasant demeanor. Life at sea had lined his face with creases. He was dressed in only cloth trousers, as Am'ayim typically did not wear shirts or shoes aboard ship. Like the first man she'd encountered, his body was covered in tattoos, and his hair and beard were similar but starting to go gray.

She smiled politely. "I assume you are the captain of this ship. I wish to secure passage to Sceotan."

The man thoughtfully thumbed one of the many earrings he wore and gazed at her with a shrewd intelligence. "Aye, wi can go dat way, but a waan expensive trip. Yuh can pay?"

Rosalie nodded politely again; thankfully this man's accent was much less pronounced. "I can pay. Who do I have the pleasure of speaking with, and when do you set sail?"

The man's smile turned crafty. "Aye, mi a di kyapten, Bez Masudo. Dis a mi ship, Di Ariela. Wi still a load, wi ago ready fi sail in a few days."

"How much for passage, food, and a cabin?"

Bez thumbed his earring again and looked over at Edmond and Jonaas. "Dem two deh a come wid yuh?"

"No, just me, those two have different paths." "Dat a still a long trip, di price a five gold marks." "I will pay you three."

The captain regarded her suspiciously. "Four marks, an yuh haffi pay one now."

Rosalie nodded. "Very well, captain, though there is one more thing.

We have a deal so long as you grant me ka'u malihini taumatau." He blinked at her and grinned. "Yuh a one smart one yes?" She held his gaze but did not reply.

"Di Ariela grant yuh ka'u malihini taumatau." Rosalie handed him a gold mark from her coin pouch, which he took with alacrity.

"I am staying at the Peddler's Respite, notify me when you and your ship are ready. Thank you Captain Masudo."

She smiled again, nodded, and had just begun to turn back to the gangway when another of the crew interrupted. This crew member was a woman. Rosalie had to blink and try not to appear startled, because the woman was also clad in only trousers. Darker skinned than the captain, she wore fewer earrings, and her short-cropped, braided hair was dyed dark purple. She was also covered in tattoos and sinewy muscles.

"Excuse mi kyapten, but di loaders dem need yuh help."

He nodded. "Tank yuh, Fatiou." He looked at Rosalie again. "Excuse mi, mi haffi attend to Di Ariela now." With that, he followed the woman across the deck.

Rosalie went to meet Edmond and Jonaas, happy to be back on solid ground. The boys were both grinning – apparently they had noticed the shirtless woman – and Rosalie had to roll her eyes. "You two are impossible."

As they started away, Rosalie stopped for the briefest of moments to watch the two boys. Edmond hit Jonaas' shoulder and they both laughed at some inane joke. She could not believe they would all be separating soon. It was going to be a hard thing, especially after leaving home and losing Crilla. She felt tears welling up again, but when Jonaas looked back at her in concern, she pulled herself together. They would be alright. All of them. They had to be.

CHAPTER SEVENTEEN:
HAVERSFJORD

Bez shook himself. He would have sworn he recognized the farm boy accompanying their new young lady passenger, but from where he couldn't say, and it gnawed at him. A cautious fellow, Bez liked to know what – and whom -- he was dealing with at all times.

Fatiou was approaching again. She had a scowl on her face, which usually meant she was dissatisfied with what the dock hands were doing. Either they were too slow, or they were being careless again. They'd already confused one load of cargo earlier, nearly costing him a fortune, but Fatiou – ever vigilant -- had caught the mistake. He thumbed his earring and smiled, lost in thought for a moment, he was surrounded by sharp women. He would need to keep an eye on the Weaver. She was one such woman, that young lady, and would need watching so no "incidents" occurred during their voyage. In that way she reminded him of his daughter which was not necessarily a good thing aboard his ship. On the other hand, he shuddered to think what any of his wives would have done to him had he refused the Weaver passage. A young lady in need was not someone you just dismissed. But it was more than that; she also wore a Weaver's ring.

Absai sidled up to Bez and spat over the gunnel into the water. "Di young lady a pay wi enough?"

Bez nodded. "Aye, shi a pay wi enough, an mi grant har ka'u malihini taumatau."

Absai blinked, obviously surprised. "How shi know bout dat? Mi no tink shi a good idea kyapten."

Bez scoffed. "Yuh neva si har Weaver's ring? Deh someting bout dis young lady.”."

Absai spat again and sighed. "Yuh rait, kyapten. Weh she ago stay wen she deh a farin?"

"Mi ago gi har mi cabin an shuffle dung di kruu."

"Aye, kyapten. Mi a go shuffle di kruu dung now."

Absai nodded and left, somewhat grumpily. Who could blame him?

He'd be sleeping in a smaller spot too.

Bez took out his paipa and lit it with his striker. He breathed deep, held his breath for a moment, then blew a cloud of haze flower smoke into the air. It was going to be a long trip to Sceotan with the young Weaver aboard.

He inhaled again as Fatiou came to stand nearby. "Weh yuh have fi mi?"

She stood tall to meet his eyes, hands behind her back, always the proper sailor. Inside, Bez chuckled ruefully. She didn't need to try so hard; she was naturally a better sailor than most of his crew.

"Di loaders dem don fi today," Fatiou went on. "Mi did tink wi shuda change some cargo fi port at Sceotan. Weh yuh tink kyapten?"

Bez nodded. "Mi tink dat a waan good idea. Di Weavers dem do like dem expensive teas an herbs."

"Mi did a tink di same ting. Di Nordrian furs food fi di trading?" "Aye, dat good. Tank yuh, Fatiou."

She saluted, fingers to lips, always the proper sailor, then went on her way.

Bez looked out over at the docks again. The town's guards were watching his ship more than the others, but he was used to it. Aedonians hated everyone who was different, profit or no. But they'd be gone in a few days anyway. He couldn't wait to be back out on the salt, away from these inland towns. He sighed and headed for his cabin to move his things.

***

Magnus picked up his ruhk, carefully considered, then placed it down before looking across the table at his opponent. "Fahz."

The boy flashed a grin then focused on the board more closely. Clearly, he didn't like to lose, and this game could possibly be Magnus' second win, evening the score at two games apiece. Since the boy, Jonaas, and his friends were leaving soon, this might be their last game. Hopefully, they'd be able to play in Kinrai during the tournament.

Jonaas moved a soldier into a blocking position, falling for Magnus' trap, and looked up. "Your move."

Magnus nodded and took a sip of his wine. "I've truly enjoyed our games and discussions over the last few days, Jonaas Al'Shane. Will I still see you in Kinrai for the tournament?"

Jonaas nodded. "That's my plan. The Weavers and the Aedonian military aren't for me, which originally left me unsure of where to go. I'd thought about following in the footsteps of my favorite author. When you told me about the tournament, I became sure of it."

Magnus winked and moved his elephant. "Fahz nihaya."

The young man blinked, checked the board and laughed. "Excellent game."

They shook hands. This Al'Shane lad was a very polite opponent and a gracious loser.

"Game five in Kinrai?" Jonaas said.

Magnus nodded. "Of course. It has been an honor playing against you these last few days." He steepled his fingers and met Jonaas' eyes. "Have you considered the offer I made to join my retinue?"

"I have. Though it's very generous of you, I want to do things on my own. I hope you understand."

"I completely understand. You take care of yourself, lad, and wish your friends well for me. I look forward to seeing you in Kinrai."

Jonaas stood. "I will do that, thank you. See you then."

As the boy walked away, Magnus leaned back, took another sip of his wine, and thought ahead to Kinrai. This year's tournament would be interesting indeed with Jonaas Al'Shane playing. Magnus might not even win this year! He laughed to think such a young boy might be his greatest adversary. How strange the world could be at times.

Aliselle Falls. That was the town Jonaas said he was from. Aliselle Falls was in the Farm Hold province. Farmers in that area were said to be relentlessly independent folk, and Jonaas certainly matched that personality. The boy had a fascinating mind. Add to that his friendship with a young Weaver and you had a very curious tale indeed. Magnus would have to visit this town on his way back home after his time in Kinrai.

***

That evening, Edmond left the inn and walked down the street. He wanted to be with his friends before they all went their separate ways, but he needed some time to think on his own too. For this reason, he had been taking these walks alone through town since they arrived a few days ago. Even this late, the town was busy. Back home the streets would be almost empty by now. But here people busily moved about the streets everywhere, going in and out of taverns, inns, shops, brothels, and the docks. If this medium-sized trade town was this busy and had this many people, he could only imagine what Bethseda must be like. He was excited to see it.

He turned aimlessly down another street. His mind consumed with the future and saying goodbye to his friends, he almost ran right into a wool merchant closing up her shop for the night.

"Sorry m'lady." He smiled and held the door for her, as her arms were filled with a load of merchandise.

The lady nodded her thanks. When she was through the door, Edmond took a deep breath and continued his walk. As he did, he paid close attention to the various townsfolk and visitors going about their evening business, and thought how amazingly different life was for people in each town.

He turned another corner and saw a commotion ahead. A small squad of Aedonian soldiers had surrounded an old man and his turnip cart. Edmond joined the crowd of onlookers to see what was happening. As he did, one of the soldiers grabbed a basket of turnips from the cart, threw it to the ground, and growled, "You gonna pay your taxes old man?"

Edmond frowned. These men didn't bear the tax collector's mark, and besides, there was no call to treat a harmless elderly man like that. He stepped into the space separating the soldiers and old man from the crowd and looked the soldier who'd thrown the basket straight in the eyes. "There's no call for that. What's going on here?"

The soldier snarled. "He hasn't paid his taxes. Mind your own business."

Edmond's eyes narrowed. "You are not tax collectors; what business is this of yours? He's just an old man trying to sell his goods."

The soldier reached for the sword at his hip. "I said to mind your own business, lad. No need to get hurt tonight."

Edmond sighed. There really was no need for this, but he wasn't going to allow them to beat an old man. He drew his sword. "I'd say you should take your own advice. I don't want to hurt any of you."

The soldier eyed Edmond's long sword cautiously, but stupidity won the night apparently. "You're just a boy, get out of here." The soldier waved his free hand dismissively. When the old man went to pick up his basket, the soldier kicked it out of his hand and laughed.

Edmond held his ground. "I won't allow you to harm an old man for no reason. Step away."

"Alright boy. I warned you!"

The soldier charged at Edmond, swinging his short sword for his side.

Edmond blocked the blow, or he meant to anyway, but his sword cleaved the soldier's blade in two. Edmond thought he saw writing of some sort on his sword for a moment, but it had never been there before and was gone just as quickly. It must have been his imagination, he focused on the fight instead. The top half of the soldier's now ruined sword fell to the ground. The soldier stumbled after it, obviously surprised. Edmond tripped him and the man fell to his knees hard.

"Now then how about the rest of you?" Edmond lifted his blade and regarded the other soldiers. They all backed away with their hands up, clearly impressed with this young man's skills.

Edmond sheathed his sword. "Get out of here and see that I don't catch you harassing any townsfolk again."

The soldiers helped their fallen man before retreating into the night.

When they were gone, Edmond helped the old man pick up his turnips then put the full basket in his cart for him.

"Thank you son, but you didn't have to do that," the old man said. "Aedonian soldiers are almost always harassing someone. It's a part of life."

Edmond frowned. " Life should be better for everyone, not just them."

The old man looked mildly confused, but he smiled and tipped his hat before climbing into his cart and snapping the reins. Edmond watched him fade into the night, then turned to face the crowd. The onlookers were dispersing now that the fighting was over. A few women at the brothel nearby waved at Edmond and gave him a "come hither" smile. Edmond smiled back but held up his hand, gently refusing them. "Peace, ladies, have a good evening!" he said and continued on his walk.

Before long, a man joined him. He was tall and older, his hair and beard gray, but he held himself straight even while clad in heavy chainmail. He carried a sword at his waist, and his blue eyes were those of an experienced warrior.

"That's quite the sword you have, son," the man commented with admiration. "Where did you get it?"

Edmond glanced at the man, sizing him up. He seemed harmless enough. Just a man trying to make conversation. "It belonged to my father."

The man nodded, though his eyes constantly surveilled the street as they walked. "I see. That is interesting. However, I would keep that to yourself and maybe not show it so boldly when you don't have to."

Edmond nodded. "That makes sense, thank you."

The man shot Edmond a sideways glance between watching the nearby alleyway they were walking past. "You know, son, normally I'd run someone into the cells for a night for scuffling with soldiers."

Edmond looked at him. "You're the town reeve? Those soldiers were hassling an old man. Maybe you should put them in your cells."

The man laughed and offered his hand. "Archibald Stallwood, reeve of Haversfjord."

Edmond respectfully took the man's hand. "I'm sorry about those soldiers, but I couldn't allow what they were doing. It was unjust."

"I agree, and I'll be making sure they understand that. You came into town with that young farmer and the Weaver, correct?"

"You noticed her ring? We don't want any trouble; we're leaving town very soon."

"Just see that you don't start any more fights, and you'll have no issues with me. Your Weaver is safe for now. Just make sure she stays inside your inn. To be sure, I have no love for the Crows."

Edmond nodded. "You have my thanks."

Reeve Stallwood continued down a different street. "Enjoy the evening son. And take good care." Edmond thought there was an odd emphasis to the man's voice, but didn't think much of it because it was probably just him being the town's reeve.

Chapter Eighteen:
How We Say Farewell

Rosalie stopped in front of the boys' door. She had seen Edmond go out for one of his evening walks and knew Jonaas was still inside. He had gone upstairs after finishing a game of Shatranj with Ser Kehlmar, and she wanted to catch him before he went on his own walk. It was frustrating, because they all used to go on evening walks together back home, but now she had to stay inside the inn alone because of all the soldiers, Jhorians, and city watch in town. Aedonia was not a friendly place for Weavers.

She went to knock but paused with her knuckles midair. Would the trick she'd thought of work? Could they be together again and not risk making a child? How sure of herself was she? She laid the palm of her hand on the door, closed her eyes and sighed. The conversation she'd had with Crilla and Gertrude weighed heavily on her mind. Yet this was her last chance to be with Jonaas in that way for perhaps a very long time, if ever. Not one to quit, she had been thinking about the problem and believed she had a solution. She needed Jonaas. She had to try.

This time she knocked. The door opened, and Jonaas stood there looking at her with those beautiful brown eyes that turned into fire under sunlight. She put her hand on his chest and rested it there for a moment, feeling his beating heart.

He touched her cheek gently. "Rosalie, what is it? Are you alright?" "Jonaas, come to my room." There, she said it!

She turned and walked ever so slowly down the hall to her own doorway. There, she waited for him, and when he had joined her, she closed the door behind them. Jonaas regarded her. His eyes held questions, but behind them was the thing she really hoped to see: the same need for her that she had for him.

"Rosalie, I want to. I really do. But we can't..."

She placed a finger over his lips, and he quieted immediately. She smiled mischievously. "I have figured out a solution for that using Weaving. Do not worry, it is not a binding Weave. Something much simpler."

That was all he needed to hear. His hands pulled her close, one wrapping around her waist and the other gently pulling her hair, tilting her face up to meet his. Their eyes met for a brief moment, but then they both closed them and kissed. She swooned against him and felt his need engulf her, as his hands started to pull her dress off. She was safe here. He loved her, and she loved him, and it was more than right that they should have one more time together before saying goodbye.

Stepping away, she smiled with all the emotion she felt for him. His eyes took on a heat, and he followed her to the bed. And there she began to weave. She gently picked him up in threads of air, removed his clothes with those same threads, and laid him on the bed. Finally, she fitted his body with a very specific and special weave. He looked at her, amused and curious, but above all, lovingly. She climbed onto him and kissed him with an insistent need of her own.

***

Later that evening, Jonaas leaned against a tree near the harbor, thinking about Rosalie. Something had changed in her since the event in the woods. She had more self-assurance, more control, and she was stronger. He liked seeing the changes – they made him worry about her less. She was becoming what he imagined the Weaver version of her would look like. (The other Weavers on Sceotan had no idea what was coming their way!) He was going to miss his friend greatly.

He pushed himself up from the tree and began walking down the street. It was getting darker and there wasn't much to see on the river anyway. Just a few ships with their night lanterns on as the last few sailors finished their day's work. The lamplighters were coming out now; he could see them here and there lighting the street lanterns. It was probably mundane to those living here, but there were no lamplighters back home and he found it interesting.

There were also patrol groups of soldiers—they called them nightwatches here—between crowds of people. Even at night Haversfjord was a busy town. He was excited to see what Kinrai, the capital city of Royal Seyla, would be like. Ser Kehlmar had told him a little about Kinrai during their games of Shatranj. Jonaas especially looked forward to seeing the different people from all over Innatraea that Ser Kehlmar told him he could expect to meet. Also, he'd have the chance to play against some real champions of Shatranj, which to him was enthralling.

He noticed two people up ahead huddled under one of the street lanterns. They appeared to be a woman and a child. A lamplighter yelled at them to move and threatened to call the watch if they didn't. Jonaas sighed. Why were so many people cruel to each other for no reason? He watched the pair, most likely mother and child, take shelter in a nearby alleyway. The child was crying and telling her mother that she was hungry.

Well, Jonaas thought, at least I can help with some things.

He went and bought a few things from a nearby food shop, then he crossed the street and bought two blankets from the wool merchant there. He had plenty of coins now, thanks to his recent games of Shatranj, and it felt good to be doing something of value with it.

He returned to the alley the woman and child had ducked down and knelt beside them. When he gently touched the woman's shoulder, she looked up at him, startled, and he got a closer look at her face. She was pretty, with light-brown wavy hair and pale gray-blue eyes. She was gaunt, probably from malnutrition, but her eyes still sparkled with life. Apparently, hope hadn't left her yet as it did with so many other people after living on the street for too long. Her daughter, unfortunately, was just as gaunt, and it made Jonaas want to cry inside. But the little girl's strange eyes, one green and one blue, shone like stars and with an intellect reminding him of Rosalie.

"It's alright," he reassured the woman. "I saw you and your child earlier. I thought you might like some food." He held out the bread, cheese, and meat he'd purchased. "It's not much, but I hope it helps you. Please take it."

The daughter grabbed the hunk of cheese and bit into it. Jonaas sighed. It was amazing how many people didn't have enough.

He laid the blankets down next to them, and the woman looked up with tears in her eyes. "I... thank you."

Jonaas nodded and smiled back. "You're welcome. Take care of yourselves." He walked away to let the woman and her daughter eat in peace.

As he made his way down the alley and back to the street, a cool breeze wafted his way. He closed his eyes and enjoyed the moment. How good it felt to help someone, even just a little.

It was probably time to head back to the inn. The night was getting darker, and the wind was picking up. He stopped and looked back at the alley. Would they be alright? He'd given them blankets, and the surrounding buildings at least blocked the wind. It would have to be enough. He couldn't do everything.

***

Niomh unfolded the two blankets and wrapped them around herself and her daughter, Aife. The night was getting colder, and the wind had picked up. So long as there was no rain they would be alright, thanks to the young stranger.

Something hard hit her foot with a clink. She reached down to see what it was, and her hand clasped around several large coins. She picked them up: gold marks. With these she and her daughter could travel to The Tanglewood and find their people! She pressed them against her forehead and cried happily, remembering all the moments of fear and sadness over her daughter's fate as they had struggled to survive. In the Danae, different colored eyes were supposed to mean the child had a great destiny. Niomh had always cried at the cruel reality that seemed to negate this myth. Now she thought maybe it was true after all. Just when she thought they were destined to die in the streets, someone had actually seen them and shown them mercy. That was a rare thing in the world outside of the Danae.

She smiled with trembling lips, tucked the coins into her empty pouch, and wiped her eyes. With this they would finally be alright.

She sat up and allowed herself to eat some of the food the young man had given them. She'd planned to save it for her daughter, even though she was starving. With these gold coins, she could afford to eat and keep up her strength for their journey.

A tiny meow made Niomh look up. A familiar white cat appeared out of the shadows. The small, spikey-haired animal had been coming to see her at night occasionally since they'd arrived in Haversfjord, but she was never able to feed it. Niomh held out a small piece of meat in her palm which the animal took quickly before scampering off into the night again.

Niomh watched the creature disappear around a corner just as the boy had. Who was that boy, anyway? No one had been that kind to them in – well, forever. In her mind she thanked him for helping get her little girl home.

She wrapped herself around Aife under their new blankets and cried softly to herself. Tomorrow there was hope.

***

Rosalie looked up as the boys sat down at her table. She had been trying to read but was being distracted by fiddling with her Weaver's ring, it was still changing subtly everyday, Crilla had told her that this was often the case with younger Weavers, because they were still forming their life's purpose. Now there were small colorful glimmers between some of the metal strands, like tiny gems waiting to be born. It was beautiful and sad too. But also gave her hope, because beauty and light were both there too. She sighed, marking her place and closing her book. Enough of that for tonight.

It would be nice to spend some time together before they all went their separate ways. They had been in Haversfjord a few days now, and she had finally gotten word from captain Masudo. It had been trying for her to be stuck inside the inn since they arrived in town, but now she had to face the aching reality of departing from her friends.

She smiled at them both, especially Jonaas. She was going to miss him so much that it actually hurt. "Hello boys, done playing outside?"

Edmond frowned as he waved one of the serving maids over. "I wouldn't call it playing. I almost had to fight a squad of watchmen who were harassing an old man."

Jonaas rolled his eyes. "I bought food and blankets for a woman and her daughter, and also gave them some extra coins. I think they were from somewhere else, maybe they can travel home now, instead of living in the streets."

The serving maid wasn't the one who usually worked at night, but she was competent. She took an order of ale and mutton for both boys—

their usual.

When she had left, Rosalie said, "Both of you promise me you will never change."

"Of course, nothing's going to change who I am," Jonaas reassured her, taking her hand in his.

Edmond puffed up his chest. "I plan on changing the world to the way I think. Those watchmen today—they should have known better than to harass an old man just trying to sell his goods. The Aedonian army needs more men like me."

Rosalie rolled her eyes, but she honestly could not wholly disagree.

Edmond was full of himself, but a good man just the same. "You are not wrong in your desire," she said, recalling something Crilla had once told her. "But remember this: an island never touches the mainland, and an Innatraean who thinks they can change the world alone is an island."

The serving maid came back with their ale and the boys took a long draft. Rosalie watched fondly and smiled. They were a pain, but she had known them her whole life, and she loved them both. Especially Jonaas. How she was ever going to get on without his beautiful smile gracing her presence every day, she didn't know.

She waited for them to put their mugs down before continuing. "I heard from Captain Masudo today. They will be ready to sail in the morning."

Jonaas set down his mug. His eyes were sad. "That soon?"

"I've been thinking," Edmond said. "We don't really know any of the people on that ship. Will you be safe?"

Jonaas smiled. Edmond was being Edmond, expecting danger around every corner. "She'll be fine. The Am'ayim would never harm a woman, let alone a Weaver."

"Jonaas is quite right," Rosalie nodded. "Plus, the captain has granted me ka'u malihini taumatau, their version of guest right. On that ship, at least, I will be safe."

"Well then," Edmond said, raising his mug, "tonight we'll stay up drinking and reminiscing and toasting our future endeavors!"

As Edmond and Jonaas knocked their mugs together, Rosalie sighed.

She was already tired, and it was late. But she would not deny her friends their last night together. Maybe she and Jonaas could have one more time alone as well. She squeezed his hand and gave him a pointed look. He smiled back, understanding in his eyes.

While the boys chatted about soldiering, Rosalie closed her eyes for a few moments, remembering Crilla and her home. She had lost them both, and in a matter of hours she would be leaving her only friends, maybe forever. Life was a very hard thing.

But then Jonaas squeezed her hand. She opened her eyes and looked into his and remembered there was joy too.

Chapter Nineteen:
The Twistings of Destiny

Archibald took off his chainmail coat and tiredly threw it on the back of his chair. He lit the candle on the small table next to it, using a striker from the Am'ayim. It caught on the first try – another wondrous item the Am'ayim traded. He used the candle to light his lantern and placed the lantern in the open study window. Finally, he sat down and poured himself a shot of whiskey.

After downing the whiskey, he set down the glass and closed his eyes. A moment of quiet was welcome in these times.

It did not last. Before long, he heard the door to his small home open and soft steps coming up the stairs. He opened his eyes in time to see the door open. The person who'd opened it threw back her invisibility cloak, revealing herself: Elspeth. The soft light flickered on her beautiful face, highlighting her strangely bright blue-green eyes. Archibald smiled.

"That is a very wide grin, old man," Elspeth said. "It has been a while, but I hope you called me here for more than entertainment."

Archibald laughed and motioned to the other chair. Elspeth sat in it and looked across the table at him.

"This isn't about getting married again is it?"

A moment of sadness came over him. He ached for this woman, but there was no changing things for now. "Of course not. I know what you're doing is more important." And he did. As far as they knew, she was the last of Trefn Cyfiawnder, or "Order of Justice," the Cathyoran order of women knights who had been annihilated years ago. Now she was slowly forming a resistance to Aedonian rule amongst the common people, an important and dangerous cause. What he had to tell her might change all of that eventually. "I saw something that might be of great interest to you today."

Elspeth looked up from the whiskey she was busy pouring for herself. "There's a boy in town who arrived a few days ago. He's accompanied by a young girl Weaver and a farm boy."

She looked at him skeptically. "Did you drink too much whiskey before lighting your lantern? I wish her well, but a young initiate Weaver cannot help us." She tossed back the shot in one gulp.

Archibald took back his glass and poured another shot for himself. "Not the Weaver. The boy" He downed the whiskey, wiped his mouth, and slapped the glass down on the table. "He's carrying the Ahearne family sword."

Elspeth sat bolt upright, her eyes wide. She took his hands in hers. "What! Are you certain?"

He looked at her reproachfully. "The hilt of his sword was wrapped to hide the family's horse head pommel, but I could tell its shape. Only one blade wielded by any man can cleave another quality sword in two. I also saw a faint glimmer of words, barely noticeable."

Elspeth stood. "Then there is hope. This changes everything. I must go see this for myself, thank you my love." She walked around the table and leaned over, kissing him hard. "I may just marry you after all."

The door downstairs slammed open, and someone came running up the stairs. Elspeth tensed, but Archibald put his hand on hers and squeezed. "It's just Kidner."

The study door opened, and a blunt, shabbily dressed man walked in.

Kidner lacked decorum, but he was smart and trustworthy. When he'd found out about Elspeth and her cause, he had offered to help rather than turn them in—a choice that might eventually cost the man his life. Earlier in the night Archibald had sent him to watch The Jhorians.

"What is it, Kidner?"

The man caught his breath before replying. "Someone informed the Jhorian's about the young Weaver. A group of them left their temple and turned toward The Peddler's Respite. There's an inquisitor with them."

Elspeth hissed and headed for the door. Archibald stood up, intending to go with her, but she shook her head at him and ran a hand down the scabbard hanging at her waist.

"Stay, my love. They may be going for the Weaver, but if they get to her our prince will be revealed too. I will stop them. We cannot risk anyone discovering our allegiance or finding the prince heir." She smiled wickedly. "Besides, it has been too long since Crogwyr got the chance to drink our enemies' blood."

With that she was gone, her cloak closing around her with its shield of invisibility.

Archibald sat back down and poured another drink. Elspeth was older now, but she would be alright. Her sword's name meant "Executioner," and for good reason. There were few alive with her skills. There would be work for him to do in the morning though, even if it was just cleaning up the corpses and apologizing to the Jhorians for their misfortune.

Kidner joined him with another glass, and they both poured a fresh drink. After draining their whiskey, Archibald sighed tiredly. "Come on, let's go. She may need us, even if she doesn't want to admit it. She's older now and it's been years since any of us have fought in a real engagement."

***

Elspeth was waiting in a side alley, trying to calm her thoughts. The Jhorians would pass right by her on their way. After this was over, she would go see the boy for herself. If he was truly wielding Dygwr Tynged, or "Fatebringer," and the sword's magic had worked, it meant he was indeed the prince heir of Cathyor. She didn't doubt Archibald—he was a smart man, and she loved him—but she had to see this for herself.

Footsteps echoed in the street, and she looked around the corner: the Jhorians. It was time.

They didn't see Elspeth as she emerged from the alleyway. Her cloak's magic, a relic of happier times, kept her from their eyes. There were four Jhorians. Two priests, a knight, and an inquisitor who was speaking to the other three as she emerged.

"Careful men, Weavers are a tricky lot, and the night belongs to them," he said. "Be on the lookout for anything."

There were certainly things in the night to be afraid of, but in this case it wasn't a Weaver. She might be older now, and the last of her order still alive, but Elspeth was strong and would protect their prince heir with her life if necessary. She could finally make good on her promise. There was hope.

She hit the two priests first, as they were the softest targets and in front. Her cloak opened with her movement, revealing herself to them as she moved. The first priest's eyes widened in surprise and what would be his final look, as Crogwyr sliced through his neck, drinking deeply of the man's blood. The blade glowed white with its plunge into the second priest's chest. She moved forward, but the knight blocked her. Their blades met, and Crogwyr glowed a brighter white—the weapon loved to make their enemies bleed.

The knight's blade was cleaved in two, rather than clanging against hers as he had on obviously expected. Shocked, he took a step back and drew the short sword still at his waist. The Inquisitor screamed, "So witch, one of you Trefn Cyfiawnder scum survived! It's no matter, we will end you tonight for what you've done to the anointed. Luvald, kill her!"

The knight drew his short sword and advanced on her like the well-trained little Jhorian slave he was. Elspeth stepped back, taking a moment to glance around and ready herself. There was no one else in sight, the few people previously there having fled at the first sign of battle.

No one in Haversfjord wanted trouble, especially when it involved the Jhorians. It wouldn't be long before the town guard or Aedonian soldiers arrived; she had to end it quickly. She raised her blade and pointed it at the knight as he moved in to engage her. He man came at her from the side, trying to jab at her quickly so he could step back and avoid her deadly sword. He probably thought it was a smart move; obviously he was still learning. It was almost unfortunate that his road would end here, but then again, it had been his choice to become a Jhorian bastard.

As the knight closed in and swung his sword, Elspeth gracefully stepped to the side and brought Crogwyr down on his arm severing it. He fell to his knees screaming. She flipped Crogwyr around and plunged the blade into the man's back. The sword's magic shone a brilliant white, as it punctured the knight's heavy armor and his heart. Elspeth drew out the blade and took a step toward the inquisitor.

"Now we end this," she said. "You are mine."

The man drew two vicious-looking long knives and smiled sadistically.

He pulled his collar down just enough to reveal the scar there. "I am Inquisitor Durand. Come, godless witch, you will not find me such easy prey!"

Recognizing the man's name and the scar on his collar bone, Elspeth felt a grim countenance spread across her face. "You were at the burning of Brynn. You killed my sisters, my queen! In Goddess Rhiannon's name I will slay you for that sin, murderer!"

She screamed and charged. But she was older and slower now and had forgotten just how dangerous this opponent might be. Jhorian inquisitors were not defenseless cowards. Rather than being cut through, his long knives blocked her blade. And in that moment of surprise, when she drew back a heartbeat slower than she should have, he struck back.

***

Inquisitor Durand pulled back his knives and retreated a step, causing a satisfying gash along the godless witch's arm. He wasn't sure what offended him more: her murder of three anointed, her belief in some archaic feminine religion, or that she thought herself his equal. He snarled. "Come witch, I will grant you the Lord's mercy, a fate too kind for the likes of you."

An experienced warrior in her situation should have shown more caution, but she screamed and came at him again, her blade going for his side. He smiled and faded to the other side just barely, bringing his knives up to feign blocking her blow. At the last moment, when her blade came into his side where it should have struck home, he moved back in, thrusting his knife into her side instead. The will of Jhoras deflected her blade from his flesh, and as her eyes opened wide in shock, his knife slid deep into her side. She cried out and he pressed his advantage. Moving forward again, he kicked her in the stomach and followed her close as her back hit the nearby alley wall. The breath was knocked out of her, and she gasped in pain. Smiling, Durand moved in close and stabbed her again.

"Now, witch, this is over. I would pray for Jhoras to show your soul mercy, but there is none for dogs like you."

"Stop right there or we will shoot!" came a shout from somewhere behind.

Durand hissed, and for a moment he thought about killing her anyway. Then again, it might be interesting to have her in chains instead.

He stepped back, pulling his knife out of her, and regarded the squad of town guards. "She attacked me and my men! Three of Jhoras' anointed have died by her hand! Arrest her!"

The town guard moved in closer, crossbows trained on the Inquisitor.

The town Reeve, Archibald Stallwood, was with them, and he looked at Durand with a grave expression.

"I don't know why you did this to your men, or who you're asking us to arrest, but it's you who will see chains tonight, Inquisitor."

"What?! She attacked us!" He looked behind him for the godless witch of a Trefn Cyfiawnder knight, but she was gone. He thrust a knife against the wall where she had been, and it hit stone. "Impossible! She was here!"

"Be that as it may, all I see now is you and a pile of corpses," Reeve Stallwood said. He looked at his men, who were still holding their crossbows on Durand. "Did you men see anyone else?"

The men shook their heads.

"I'm sure the church can sort this out in the morning, but tonight you are under arrest, Inquisitor," Reeve Stallwood said. He nodded toward the guardsmen. "I'd advise you to come quietly unless you want to join those poor souls."

Durand dropped his knives and let Reeve Stallwood and his men take him into custody. He didn't know how the godless witch had escaped him, but her time would come. He was a patient man, and he had seen her face. She would die for her sins. The anointed of Jhoras always achieved justice against the godless.

***

The next morning Jonaas woke early and headed for the docks. He wanted to stretch his legs before meeting his friends. There were more soldiers than usual patrolling the streets, but none of them paid him any mind, and he reached the docks in good time.

The ship Rosalie would be taking to Sceotan was a pretty vessel, all dark wood and hold gilded trim, with a lion as her figurehead. Examining it from the dock below, he hoped she sailed as well as she looked. The sailors and their captain were already up and checking everything before setting sail. He also noticed a squad of soldiers keeping watch. Apparently, they weren't fans of Am'ayim, but their trade was lucrative enough to hold off actual hostilities. Jonaas shook his head. It seemed most Aedonians were hostile toward nearly everyone. What was it that made people from Aliselle Falls so different?

Someone he recognized was approaching the ship's captain. It was the woman he'd helped last night, accompanied by her daughter. He smiled. Hopefully she was going home. He knew well how hard it was to be far away from family. He had guessed she was from another land based on how she looked, and that was why he'd hidden the gold marks in her blankets. It made him happy to know that he'd truly helped them.

A familiar voice nearby said, "Are they the woman and child you rescued last night?"

Jonaas looked and saw Rosalie coming up beside him. "They are, I'm just happy to see them leaving. I was hoping they would."

Rosalie smiled warmly. "I am going to miss your kindness. Never change."

Edmond joined them, and the three huddled close for a long time, reminiscing and laughing at the things they'd done as children not so long ago. Finally they broke apart and stood back looking at each other. Jonaas still found it hard to believe they were actually parting ways. These two had always been in his life, especially Rosalie. He'd loved her their entire childhood. Her power scared him, but he knew her heart. Inside she was just a normal girl like everyone else. "Will you be alright?" he asked her.

Rosalie smiled sadly. "I will be fine, Jonaas, I promise." She closed her eyes for a brief moment. "Crilla prepared me for this my whole life. I can do it. I should go, the captain will be waiting for me. You two will be alright. Do not do anything stupid without me around."

Jonaas grinned. "We will be alright. We're leaving today as well." Edmond nodded. "That's the plan."

She straightened Edmond's shirt and looked him in the eyes one more time. "Goodbye, Edmond. I am sure we will meet again."

"Goodbye Rosalie. You want to dunk me in the harbor for the memories?"

She hugged him and patted his cheek. "Do not tempt me."

Now she looked at Jonaas, and her eyes became sensitive pools of emotion. They went into each other's arms and embraced tightly, each reluctant to let the other go. When they eventually did, Jonaas could see that her eyes had welled up with tears. He felt his own eyes growing moist. "You can do this," he told her. "You're stronger than anyone I know."

They pressed their lips together in a desperate last effort to express how they felt.

"I will always love you too," she said caressing his cheek. "Take care of yourself Jonaas. Be safe and come see me when you can.”

He nodded. “I promise.”

“Goodbye, both of you. Stay true to yourselves. Hopefully we will meet again one day soon. May the Goddesses keep you both safe until then.”

“Stay true, Rosalie,” Edmond said. “And give them hell.”

Jonaas tried to smile but he hurt too much. “Goodbye, Rosalie. I love you and always will. Take good care, and always remember us.”

Standing together on the dock, Edmond and Jonaas watched Rosalie walk away. The first few steps seemed hard for her, and when she stopped to look back, they smiled encouragingly. She smiled too, her usual confident self. Then she turned away and walked on. By the time she reached the ship’s gangway, her strides had lengthened to a more normal pace. She boarded the vessel and gave one last wave to the boys.

She was really going.

Jonaas felt an ache in his chest, but he was happy she was on her way to becoming who she was. “Maybe we should go with her,” he sighed. “She’ll be alright won't she Edmond?”

Edmond turned to him and laughed. “She’ll be running that tower in a year. It’s us I’m worried about.”

Epilogue: Questions

The My'yh was furious. A few days earlier she had been told what to do. (No one told her what she was *supposed* to do—she was not a child to be ordered about on the whims of others.) She bit her lip, her mind reeling.

The request (she refused to call it a command) had come from The Three Sisters. Innatraea's goddesses had told her, in no uncertain terms, to pay attention to a specific young boy, to learn about him, and should she find the boy worthy, allow him access to Haitasi. She was angry but also curious. What kind of Innatraean was he that those three would tell her to observe him and allow him into her home? But she had done as "requested," and observed him, this Jonaas Al'Shane. Still, she didn't understand. The situation was completely unacceptable.

It didn't make sense any way she looked at it. This Al'Shane boy simply didn't belong. He was a puzzle, and the My'yh didn't like puzzles. The young girl who could Weave, on the other hand, did make sense. She was powerful, raised by a most impressive woman, and touched by The Three Sisters. The boy warrior—Edmond was his name—also had a somewhat impressive history. An ancient relic for a sword, the son of a king, and connected to the old world. But this farm boy? Who was he? Why did he belong?

The My'yh moved her hand over the world pool before her, watching the ripples spread across its surface at her will. Time seemed to flow backward before her gaze, tracing the young man's life from the present back to his childhood and eventually his birth. A tragedy. His mother had been attacked, had been taken away from her people, and died giving birth to this seemingly unexceptional young man. Half Rinowhn, raised on a simple farm and possessing no power in a strict sense. Yet he was intimately connected to so many who had, or would, change Innatraea in their own way. A woman who did not age. A retired soldier who sought peace. A Weaver who left their order rather than giving up her beliefs. A young prince, unaware of his identity yet tied to the past by his father's sword. A young woman, stolen at birth, found and adopted. The most powerful Weaver ever born.

Then there was this young farm boy. Why could she not see his future? She paused, her hand hovering over an interesting moment: the first time he beat his adoptive father at Shatranj. How had such a young child, who lacked training and didn't have a leader's experience or a fighter's will, become such a master of the ancient game? The My'yh chained that moment to her mind then moved her hand again, observing all his games. In the last few he stood on even ground with an experienced knight, war leader and champion of Shatranj. It was interesting, but not an answer of its own.

The book. A one of a kind tome that detailed nearly every land and culture across Innatraea. It was also interesting because somehow she wasn't familiar with its author, this Tavid the Traveler. He also bore his mother's pendant, a Zuniga stone of the Zimsway Rinowhn, though he had no idea what that actually meant. There were too many questions surrounding this young man for her to simply pass him by. A puzzle with influence upon the threads of so many destined souls wasn't something she could ignore; it was intriguing and possibly dangerous.

She paused her hand, as his face rippled into her vision on the pool's surface. Who are you Jonaas Al'Shane? Why do you belong with them?

Why can I not see your future? She hissed in annoyance, a rare thing. Then, in a moment of decision, she moved her hand away allowing the pool to become peaceful again. She would call him; fate and destiny required answers.

She began to chant. *"Come to me, my lost one…"*

***

Elspeth woke with a start and tried to sit up but fell back gasping in pain and closing her eyes again. A hand gently but firmly rested on her shoulder, squeezing comfortably, and Archibald's familiar voice spoke. Why did it always have to be him? She loved him, he'd been at her side since the fall of Cathyor and the death of everything she had held dear, but it wasn't easy to admit she needed a man to save her. And he had saved her so many times throughout the years.

"Rest, my love," Archibald's soothing voice insisted. "You were gravely injured, we almost lost you. Thankfully, Fletcher knows his craft well."

Memories flashed through her mind, and her eyes shot open. "The boy, our prince, is he alright?" She tried to sit up, a feeling of dread taking over, but that damned hand kept her laying down far too easily.

Archibald smiled kindly. "All is well. He and the other one left town a few days ago, just after the young girl Weaver sailed away on an Am'ayim ship."

She tried to sit up again, but the hand was still there. Her stomach and sides screamed in pain. "I have to follow. If he's truly our prince, I must find him and keep him safe!"

"You can follow him when you're healed. I will accompany you. A few of your people as well. The boy is strong, he's survived this long. Patience my love."

"My people! I need to tell them what happened!"

"Rest easy, I already sent Kidner to tell them. I know you."

Hearing the name of the man she'd only met recently made her nervous. "Kidner?"

"I trust him. He knows where to find them and what to say."

Elspeth suddenly felt exhausted and she closed her eyes. It had been so long since she faced an inquisitor. Once, she would have stood on even ground with him, but she had lost this fight before it even began. For nearly two decades she had been building a resistance, leading them in small raids against their enemy and teaching them to fight. She wasn't just a warrior any longer but a leader, the last of her sisters, a final light in the dark. Tears fell down her cheeks. She couldn't afford to be soft. She had to find the boy and defeat those who had taken the life of her queen and those of her sisters so long ago.

She desperately reached out, pulling on Archibald's sleeve. Her eyes opened, and she met his gaze with determination. "Promise me, Archibald. That we will find him, that you'll come with me, and we will make them pay for what they took from us. Promise me." Her voice sounded much shakier than she'd intended.

His hand rested over hers and squeezed firmly. "We will, I promise you."

She saw the same determination in his eyes. Archibald was a man, and could never truly understand what she had lost, but he was also Cathyoran deep in his soul. Elspeth closed her eyes and drifted into darkness.

GLOSSARY

Absai (Ab-eh-sigh): An officer aboard The Ariela.

Aedonia (Ah-doh-nee-uh): A kingdom in eastern Innatraea, bordering the Mu'ul Mountains. Known to conquer and absorb smaller nations, charge heavy taxes, enact strict laws, and is also home to the Holy Church of Jhoras.

Ahearne Family: (Ah-hear-neh): The ruling family of Cathyor before the kingdom's fall. History says that they were all slain with their kingdom.

Aife (Ai-fe): Niomh's daughter, who is unusual because she has two different colored eyes, one blue and one green.

Aliselle Falls (Al-eh-see-ill): A farm town near the eastern border of Aedonia. It's located in the province of Farm Hold and named after the river rapids, and waterfalls nearby.

Amah (Ahm-ah): A Weaver of Tursi descent, long dead, she wrote a book "The Morals of the Weave," which is still referenced by many Weavers to this day.

Amarok (Ahm-ah-rok): A Sacred Folk race that is said to resemble giant wolves.

Am'ayim, "People of Sea Mist," (Am-eye-eem): The people of the Ara'ayim isles.

Amng (Ahm-uhng): One of the two peoples native to Amng'khor. Andalus (An-dahl-us): A kingdom in westwern Innatraea.

Andalan (An-dahl-un): The people native to Andalus.

Amng'Khor (Ahm-uhng-kore): The southern kingdom of the far east. Known for hot jungles, spicy foods, ancient temples, and strange animalistic based religions.

Ara'ayim Isles, "Islands of Sea Mist," (are-ah-eye-eem): Home of the Am'ayim. The isles are located far off the western coast. Outsiders are only allowed on the few larger islands outside the central waterway of the isles.

Archibald Stallwood (Arch-ih-bald Stall-wood): The town reeve of Haversfjord.

The Ariela, "Lioness of the Sea," (Are-Ee-el-ah): An Am'ayim trade ship, captained by Bez Masudo.

Asherah, "Lady of the Sea," (Ash-err-ah): The mother goddess of Innatraea, who gave birth to The Three Sisters.

Asherah Tree (Ash-err-ah): An ancient mythological species of tree that is the symbol of Asherah. They are believed to have provided the seeds which gave birth to Innatraea.

Barth (Bart): A criminal on the King's Highway.

Bay of Swans: The massive bay near Royal Seyla's capital city of Kinrai. Bethseda (Beth-said-ah): The capital city of Aedonia.

Bezalel "Bez" Masudo (Bez-zuh-lel Muh-soo-doh): Captain of The Ariela.

The Bond: A lifelong magical connection between Weaver and their personal Goddess Bound. It grants increased strength, faster healing, and slower aging. But it also instills a desire to obey their Weaver on all things.

Brianna Carlon (Bree-ahn-nuh Car-lawn): Edmond's grandmother.

Cathyor (Kath-yore): One of the last ancient kingdoms. Conquered by Aedonia some years ago.

Chaya (Chai-uh): A woman of the Zimsway Rinowhn. Rescued by the Al'Shane family after being attacked. She died giving birth to Jonaas.

Closed Consensus: A meeting in the Great Loom, of only the Greater Consensus.

Clyde (Klai-duh): A criminal on the King's Highway.

Crawley Family (Craw-lee): Family friends of the Al'Shanes. Robert, his wife Laura, and their daughter Maryanne. Robert also has a sister named Alaina.

Crilla Sharone (Krill-ah share-ohn-ay): A retired Weaver of legendary status. Gertrude Al'Shane's sister. Crilla became Rosalie Sharone's adoptive mother after finding her abandoned as a baby.

Crogwyr, "Executioner," (Cog-wee-ah): Elspeth Anwyl's sword. Crows: Nickname for The Jhorian Crows.

Danae (Dan-ay): The semi-nomadic people who inhabit the outskirts of the vast Tanglewood. They can also be found in small numbers throughout many other kingdoms.

Brother Deniz (Den-izz): A Weaver of Tursi heritage.

Daphne (daf-nee): The Dryad connected to the Great Tree known as the Shepherd King.

Devori Mountains (Dev-oh-rye): The mountains surrounding Sophene, the eastern border of what used to be Thava, The Rinowhn Tribelands, and The Great Rift.

Djelem'den, "Pedestal of the World" or "Garden Tower," (Gel-em-den): The giant tower home of The Weavers.

Dragon Wall: A mountain range making up the northern border of Farundia.

Dryad: A Sacred Folk race. These giant feminine titans share a spiritual bond with Innatraea's Great Trees and are able to traverse between Innatraea and the spirit world known as Kanraphim.

Inquisitor Durand (Dur-and): An inquisitor of the Holy Church of Jhoras.

Dygwr Tynged, "Fatebringer," (Dye-wee-ah Tin-yed): The Ahearne Family Sword, known to have a horse head shaped pommel. Unique among Trefn Cyfiawnder swords because its magic can be used by a man of the Ahearne Family.

Edmond Carlon (Ed-mond Car-lawn): Childhood friend to Rosalie and Jonaas, Brianna's grandson.

Elspeth Anwyl {Els-peth Ann-wh-eel): A former member of Cathyor's Trefn Cyfiawnder.

Sister Evelyn Atwood (Ev-vel-lyn At-wood): A Weaver of Aedonian heritage. Priestess of Initiates and a member of the Greater Consensus.

Fahz (Fah-zz): A phrase in Shatranj, indicating a threat on your opponent's shah.

Fahz Nihaya (Fah-zz Nee-high-uh): A phrase in Shatranj indicating your opponent's shah is threatened and has no escape. Game end.

Farm Hold: A province in Eastern Aedonia known for farm towns.

Farundia (Far-un-dee-ah): The kingdom which makes up the southwest isthmus of the continent. A land known for its juxtaposition between the rich and powerful cities around various Oasis and the mountain borders versus the savage nomadic tribes that wander its vast deserts.

Farun Da'al (Far-un-dahl): The capital city of Farundia. Farundian (Far-un-dee-ann): The people of Farundia. Fatiou (Fat-ee-ow): An officer aboard The Ariela.

Fletcher (Fletch-ur: The town doctor of Haversfjord. River of Flowers: A river in northern Royal Seyla.

Brother Frederick Alwin (Fred-ur-ick All-win): A Weaver of Aedonian heritage. A member of The Greater Consensus.

Gertrude Al'Shane (Gur-true-de Al-sheyn): Jonaas' adoptive mother, wife to Jonathan, and sister to Crilla Sharone.

Glow Orb: An orb made of bent light, created by Weavers. They can vary in size, and color, drastically. They can also be moved about at the creator's will.

Goddess Bound: The elite irregular military organization that acts as personal bodyguards for individual Weavers. Known for The Bond, a lifelong magical connection granting increased strength, faster healing, and slower aging; which also instills a desire to obey the Weaver on all things.

The Great Loom: The vast chamber in the upper floors of Djelem'den. It is used for meetings of the Greater and Lesser Consensus.

The Greater Consensus: The ruling body of The Weavers. This council is always composed of thirteen full Weavers, though it's rare that all of them are publicly known.

The Great Rift: A massive rift in the Devori Mountains. It borders Sophene, The Rinowhn Tribelands, and what used to be the border of Thava.

Great Tree: The commonly used moniker referring to any of the ancient giant trees around Innatraea. Most of these have specific names and tower over their surroundings, whether near cities or even mountains.

Haitasi, "The Stones," (Hai-tai-see): The My'yh's realm. Legend says that the stones here allow travel through time and location.

Hakob (How-cub): A Sophenen man who died centuries ago, of old age. Crilla Sharone's first love.

Haversfjord (Hav-urs-fyord): A large Aedonian rivertrade town on the King's Highway.

Haze Flower: A psychoactive plant. It can be identified by its colorful large flower buds and multipoint leaves. It is a very popular trade commodity, in many forms, across Innatraea.

The Holy Church of Jhoras (Jo-ras): The official church of Aedonia. It's known for strong military, harsh judgements, political power, wealth, and hatred of those that challenge it. The Holy Church has a long history of oppressing women's power and conflicts with The Weavers.

Imperial Shinoda (Shin-oh-duh): The northern kingdom of the far east. Little is known of this kingdom as it is isolated from the rest of the continent by the treacherous Mu'ul mountain range.

Innatraea (Ee-nah-tray-uh): The known world.

Innatraean (Ee-nah-tray-uhn): The human folk of the known world.

Jhoras (Jo-ras): The one God of the Holy Church of Jhoras.

Jhorian Crows (Jo-ree-an): The left arm, inquisitors and exorcists, of the Holy Church of Jhoras.

Jhorian Phalanx (Jo-ree-an): The mighty right arm, or military, knights of the Holy Church of Jhoras.

Jonaas Al'Shane (Jo-nus Al-Sheyn): Childhood friend of Edmond and Rosalie.

Jonathan Al'Shane (Jaa-nuh-thn Al-Sheyn): Jonaas' adopted father,

Gertrude's husband.

Kanraphim (Kan-ruh-fim): The spirit world and or afterlife. The actual beliefs vary drastically between different kingdoms and people.

Khor River (Kore): A river in Amng'khor.

Khoran (Kore-ann): One of the two peoples native to Amng'khor.

Kievan (Key-vahn): A kingdom, and people by the same name, in western Innatraea.

Kidner (Kid-nehr): A man who works for Reeve Stallwood in Haversfjord.

The King's Highway: The large, well maintained and guarded, trade road that runs through Aedonia. From the northern Jhorian coastal trade city Porto de la Luce, through the kingdom's capital city of Bethseda, and all the way south to the border of Royal Seyla.

Kinrai (Kin-rye): The capital city of Royal Seyla.

Kievan (Key-von): A kingdom in western Innatraea that borders Sophene. Its people go by the same name as their kingdom.

River of Kings: A large river that flows through Aedonia from its northern coast near Porto de la Luce.

Legacy: A new Weaver initiate who is sponsored by a current, or retired, Weaver. Many times they are the sponsor's child.

Lesser Consensus: The collective body of all Weaver's on Sceotan at any given time. They often have input on important matters but it is the Greater Consesus who makes all final decisions.

Luau River (Loo-ah-oo): A river in Amng'khor.

Magnus Kehlmar (Mag-nus kell-mar): A knight lord of Aedonia. He is known as a master player of the strategy game Shatranj.

Marged Llewellyn (Mar-ged Luh-wel-in): One of the few survivors of Trefn Cyfiawnder. She lives in Aliselle Falls with her two husbands Brandon, and Rory. She helped train Edmond Carlon.

River Marnah (Mar-nuh): A river in The Rinowhn Tribelands.

Mundukua, "World Pool," (Moon-doo-koo-ah): An ancient magical artifact that appears to be a pool of water. They allow visions of different locations and forms across Innatraea.

Mu'ul Mountains (Mewl): A treacherous mountain range that divides central Innatraea from the east, bordering Aedonia. There are a few nomadic tribes that live in these harsh climbs, mostly looked at as raiders and slave traders.

The My'yh (Mai-yah): A Sacred Folk race and singular individual of incredible power. The guardian of Haitasi.

Niomh (Nee-ohm): A Danae woman living on the streets of Haversfjord with her daughter Aife.

Nordria (Nor-dree-uh): A distant northern kingdom of harsh mountains and ice. Made of different regions ruled by many different clans.

Praeus (Pray-us): An ancient Weaver of unknown descent. Though long dead his name is still often spoken because of his book "The Linguistics of Logic and Power," which is still respected to this day.

Paipa (Pie-puh): Am'ayim word for a smoking pipe.

Porto de ła Luce, "Light's Port," (Por-toe-dey-lah-loos): Aedonia's large northern coastal trade city. Known as the seat of power of The Holy Church of Jhoras.

Renfal Forest (Rinn-fawl): The Forest around Aliselle Falls.

Rhiannon, The Great Horse Queen (Ree-an-non): One of the Three Sisters. Goddess of the moon, wealth, power, and fertility.

Rinowhn Tribes (Rin-oh-in): The native peoples of the Rinowhn Plains.

The Rinowhn Tribelands, or "Sea of Grass," (Rin-oh-in): The vast grassland plains, mountains, and valleys that make up most of central Innatraea. Outsiders are strongly discouraged from visiting for very long by the tribes.

Rosalie Sharone (Row-zuh-lee share-ohn-ay): Childhood friend of Jonnas and Edmond, adopted daughter and Legacy of retired Weaver Crilla Sharone.

Rose Apple: A hard to grow variety of apple that tastes similar to a pear. There are many ancient rose apple orchards near Aliselle Falls.

Royal Seyla (Say-lah): A kingdom in southeastern Innatraea. Known for being one of the richest kingdoms on Innatraea, to be supportive of artists and scholars, and as home of the strategy game Shatranj.

Sacred Folk: The collective moniker for any of the ancient mythical non-Innatraean races of Innatraea. The actual number of different races, and how many are still surviving, is unknown. There are many stories about their magical powers and origins, that vary greatly between regions and race.

Sceotan (skay-oh-tan): Island kingdom of the Weavers. Located off the southern coast of Innatraea.

Sceotian (Skay-ocean): The native people of Sceotan.

Selene, The Moon Dog (Sell-een): One of the Three Sisters. Goddess of transition, roads, and the night.

Ser (Sehr): Honorific given to an Aedonian knight and lord.

Seraphina, The Fire Snake (Sehrah-fee-nuh): One of The Three Sisters. Goddess of fire, light, passion, and rage.

Serra (Sehr-ah): Jonaas Al'Shane's donkey. Seylan (Say-lawn): The people of Royal Seyla.

Shepherd King: A Great Tree in Aedonia, bordering The King's Highway.

Shatranj (Shuh-traanj): An ancient, and very popular, game of strategy; which is played on a wooden board between two opponents.

Sister Sherielle Arsenault: A Weaver of Nordrian heritage. She is a member of The Greater Consensus.

Siofra (She-fra): A Sacred folk race known to swap human babies for their own changeling infant children.

Siua River (See-oo-ah): A river in Amng'khor.

Skywalk: A fortified city in the Dragon Wall, that yards Farundia's northern border.

Sister Solange Mason (Sol-aanj may-sun): A Weaver of Seylan heritage.

Sophene (So-feen): A mountainous kingdom in western Innatraea, that borders Kievan.

Sophenen (So-fin-inn): The native people of Sophene.

Sister Taia Mirzoyan (Tie-uh mirz-oh-yan): A Weaver of Sophenen heritage. A member of The Greater Consensus, and an old friend of Crilla Sharone.

Talberston's Crossing (Tahl-burr-stuns): A river town in Aedonia.

The Tanglewood: A vast southern coastal forest on the border of Royal Seyla, Aedonia, and the Rinowhn Tribelands. Rumors about it abound, from strange creatures, hidden cities, and magic. TlMany of the Danae people live on its outskirts.

Tavid the Traveler (Tav-eed): A book written by a man of the same name. The book details his many travels throughout Innatraea as well as cultural and historical information on nearly every kingdom and people, including Sacred Folk.

Teokahl (Tay-oh-kahl): Capital city of Amng'Khor.

Thane Family (Thayn): Family friends of the Al'Shanes. Jacob, his wife Alice, and their daughter Rebecca.

Thava (thaw-vah): A once great alliance of kingdoms that took up most of northwestern Innatraea. It has now been split up into its original smaller kingdoms, one of which is Sophene.

Three Sisters: The daughters of Asherah. Rhiannon, Selene, and Seraphina. Innatraea's three sister goddesses and moons.

Tursim (Tur-seem): A very large city state bordering the Tanglewood and the Rinowhn Tribelands where the Victory River meets the sea. It is the largest and richest trade city on the Innatraea.

Tursi (Tur-see): The native people of Tursim.

Victory River: The large river, big enough ships tomeasuly sail, that spns Innatraea from north to south. Most of the river lies with Aedonia's borders.

The Weavers: An ancient organization made up of those who can Weave from all over Innatraea.

Weaving: The innate ability to see the threads of magical power that make up innatraea and manipulate them at will. It is a rare trait few are born with.

Weavers' Rings: An often threaded and gemmed ring made from unknown elements; they are also the identifying mark of a Weaver to normal Innatraeans. It is believed that each ring is unique to its wearer, the threads, symbols, or gems meaning something. They have also been rumored to change over time along with their Weaver throughout life. But in truth little is known about these mysterious artifacts.

Zimsway Rinowhn (Zims-way Rin-oh-in): One of the Rinowhn tribes. They are known as Innatraea's predominant experts in Haze Flower farming.

Zuniga Stone (Zuh-nee-gah): Rough stone pendants line with veins of blue, hold, and purple; somehow connected to the Zimsway Rinowhn.

Novella Two Preview:

House Masudo

Decades earlier...

Bez tried to calm himself, which wasn't easy given the circumstances. He swallowed, mouth feeling dry, as her hand reached down to pick up one of the perfume jars. He'd first met her last night, when he and his younger friend Absai had gone to a local tavern, and like an idiot, he'd flirted with and bedded her before knowing who she was. Now this was his reward, a glorious fate, if it wasn't such a terrible joke.

Bez had heard the Masudo women were crazy, but he'd never

expected one to be at a tavern drinking and dancing. He sighed, watching her lift the clear glass jar off his cart, and looked up, meeting her eyes. Tiare Masudo, sister to Ni'moku's matriarch, regarded him evenly. Her deep brown eyes said everything; she could feel the difference in weight.

Her gaze held him like a vice. He may as well have been chained before her like a slave, which he still might be. He couldn't help but remember the previous evening—the dancing, the alcohol, and her lithe, muscular body against his. The House Masudo tattoo on her side seemed to glow in the bright sunlight. He had somehow missed it last night, and now he was paying for that mistake. To think he had been happy at first, when the woman from last night had appeared at the docks, watching him. He forced himself to look away from her tattooed body and back into her eyes. She smiled, noting where his eyes had been, while opening the perfume bottle and pouring its contents on the ground. The sensuous smell of musk, lily, and vanilla came to his nose as the blue sapphires hit the sandy gravel by his boots.

To the community that helped make Innatraea possible, thank you.

Peter, Vesna, Manca, Julija, GiGi, Pouchi, Jeanine, Jean-Paul, Fil, Hétu, Irak, Marian M., George M., Todd M., Jason Bratt, Justin Bratt, C.M., Spencer P., Moriah C., Vanessa C., Brandon H. Westmoreland, Jim Chabot, Anne Chabot, Samantha Hopkins, Ron, Elaine, John, Justin, Jacob, Lori Crutchfield, Dusty Ranger, Michael B., Dawne M. Mitchell, Nathaniel L. Glenn, Lincoln Escandon, G. Reyes, Sam J., N.C., Michael Kantor,

Learn more about Innatraea!

www.innatraea.com

ABOUT THE AUTHOR

E.R. Zaugg has published several articles on being the parent of a vulnerable child, won poetry contests, and been an avid reader and world traveler for decades. His work is inspired by seeing the world and encountering different religions, spiritual beliefs, and cultures in both literature and actual journeys. These experiences have led to a body of deeply poetic work that explores what it means to be human. The Innatraea novella series highlights the value of vulnerable cultures, children, and strong women, with the goal of imparting to its readers a greater understanding and love of humanity.